DREAM WALKER

BOOK TWO

WIDE AWAKE IN DREAMLAND

G.W. Mullins

LIGHT OF THE MOON PUBLISHING

Mullins

© 2022 by G.W. Mullins

ISBN: 978-1-7377100-4-2

First Printing

This is a work of fiction. Names, characters, businesses, places, events and incidents are either the products of the author's imagination or used in a fictitious manner. Any resemblance to actual persons, living or dead, or actual events is purely coincidental.

Light Of The Moon Publishing has allowed this work to remain exactly as the author intended, verbatim, without editorial input.

Printed in the United States of America

For further information, on his writing, visit G.W. Mullins' web site at http://gwmullins.wix.com/books

Also Available from G.W. Mullins in Hardback, Paperback and eBook

Rise Of The Snow Queen
Book Two:
The War Of The Witches

What begins as a simple, bittersweet tale about a man turned into a polar bear, grandly unfolds into a rich, mythical adventure in the best-selling book series Rise Of The Snow Queen. Based on Hans Christian Andersen's fairy tale, author G.W. Mullins expands on this story creating a new mythology that takes readers into the world of snow and ice.

In part two, the story develops long before the adventures of Gerda and Kai. It takes readers to a remote mountain village where winter claims lives at the Snow Queen's command. The story goes back to the Mirror and how it cracked, sending its shards into the world to infect the innocent. This take on the story, embarks on a much more adult tone with the mood turning rather sinister as the Snow Queen battles to obtain the mirror and rule them all. Rise Of The Snow Queen Two - War Of The Witches, is a dark fairy tale that unfolds to a conclusion you won't expect to see coming.

Rise Of The Snow Queen Book One: The Polar Bear King

The first book from the new "Rise Of The Snow Queen" four part series.

G.W. Mullins has taken timeless folklore and crafted it into a new book series meant for adults. His updated take on the Polar Bear King and Snow Queen pay homage to the stories we all loved as children while making them more adventurous and not always allowing for a "happily ever after" ending.

The newly crowned King Valeman refuses to marry an evil witch, who reveals herself to be the infamous Snow Queen. His refusal to align himself with the dark forces causes her to cast an enchantment upon him.

Her unbreakable spell changes him beyond belief. "By light one way, by night another. Your form will change you will soon discover. By day a beast of a bear you will be, at night a man while others sleep. To break this spell you much achieve, the love of another while being a beast."

Valeman is transformed into the Polar Bear King and given seven years to find true love or the enchantment will be permanent.

***Daniel Awakens
A Ghost Story
Begins***

***Death Is Only
The Beginning***

Author G.W.
Mullins turns
back time in his
Best-Selling
"From The Dead
Of Night" book
series.

In Daniel
Awakens A Ghost
Story Begins, Mullins takes you back to the day
Daniel died. In a welcome addition to the fan
favorite series, readers will learn what happened to
Daniel.

Daniel had known his whole life something was not
right. He never connected with the woman who he
was told was his mother. As his sixteenth birthday
approached, he learned the life he had lived was
based around a hidden past. His worst suspicions
were realized when the truth of his father's affair
came to light. As Daniel ran from the house of lies,
he had no idea his young life was about to end.

Daniel awakened in the cemetery, and quickly came to learn death is only the beginning. Thrust into a world of the undead, he had no time to learn of the afterlife or the battle of good and evil. The dark ones were coming, whether he was ready or not, he would soon learn of the dark-lighters and a force of evil named Malachi.

Destined to be a leader in the fight for the balance of power, Daniel is thrust into a battle he is not ready for. He quickly learns of his abilities and the lack of experience he has to control them. Daniel must fight to save the force of good.

***Daniel's Fate
A Ghost Story
Ends
"From the Dead
Of Night" Book
Four***

***Daniel walked
in the land of
the Dead. Now
the Dead want
him back.***

As the dark ones came for Daniel, he was forced to take refuge in the light, the last place he wanted to be. There, he was to decide his own fate. Staying in the light and ascending meant

Jen would be left defenseless. If he chose being human again, the dark ones would have the

power to take over the world. As Daniel made his decision, the dead began to rise. The dark

ones were coming forward to block the light and create hell on earth.

Death is only the beginning... From The Dead Of Night Book 4

Daniel Is Waiting A Ghost Story "From the Dead Of Night" Book One

Daniel walked in the land of the dead. Now the dead want him back!

The veil is lifted between the living and the dead as the Shadows come forward to capture him.

Daniel Stratton died in a tragic accident. His life should have been over but it was not. His spirit spent the next sixty years trying to communicate with the people who came to the cemetery where he was entombed. Then Jen came one night to the mausoleum seeking refuge from a life that was spinning out of control. There she found Daniel.

As they work together to free him from his forced confinement; they learn that the Light comes for all dead, and Daniel is forced to enter it. In his case there is no matter of choice. Inside he fights for his life and escapes but the enforcers of the light come for him. He saw seven of these shadow people within the light and each marked him. Daniel knows these Shadows will come for him. Each one of the seven will take the body of a human who had just succumbed to death turning them to Zombie like creatures to do their bidding.

Together Daniel and Jen must confront the "Shadows" so that they can survive to see another day.

***Daniel Returns
A Ghost Story
"From The
Dead Of Night"
Book Two***

Daniel walked in the land of the dead. Now the dead want him back!

The story continues where

"Daniel Is Waiting A Ghost Story" ended in a cliff hanger.

 Daniel died a tragic death and should be dead. He walked in the land of the dead for too long. Then the light came for him but he refused it. He fought to escape it, but higher powers had other plans for him.

His fate was to ascend and take on the role of angel, but something went wrong. Before he could assume his role, he met Jen. When Daniel fought the light to stay with Jen, he broke the law of the dead. Within the light seven Shadow enforcers saw him. They reached out to stop him and in doing so marked him. When Daniel escaped, he knew the seven would come for him.

The forces of good and evil watch to see who can claim Daniel in the end and control the ultimate power that is growing within him.

Messages From The Other Side Stories of the Dead, Their Communication, and Unfinished Business

Best-selling author G.W. Mullins shares his personal journey towards understanding death, the afterlife and communication with spirits of loved ones who have passed over. In "Messages From The Other Side Stories of the Dead, Their Communication, and Unfinished Business," Mullins tells of dealing with the grief of his mother passing and the reassurance of an after death communication that totally changed his outlook towards death and grief.

This book not only tells of Mullins' personal journey into understanding but also guides others to understand why we receive communications and the signs to look for. Mullins also explores visitation dreams and tells of his own personal experience in the area and shares the stories of others who have had similar experiences.

This book highlights the author's personal journey in an exploration for knowledge, and his understanding, without question, there is life after death. Mullins invites you to join him on this journey through life and death.

Vengeance
A Paranormal
Murder Mystery

"Mystery, Murder, Paranormal Events, and a story that leaves you guessing as the bodies stack up."
– Matthew Trent OutLoud Magazine

After the death of her father, Danni starts a new life in a seaside town in New York where she and her mother move into a strange Gothic house with a terrible history. From the moment Danni gets there, she feels she is being watched. She is sure they are not alone in the house.

As Danni learns of her new home, she is told of a past resident who fell to her death on the nearby cliffs at the same time that her teenaged daughter, Elizabeth, disappeared.

Elizabeth's spirit, appears to Danni and claims that her mother's death was a murder, not suicide and asks for Danni's help in bringing the dangerous killer to justice.

The mystery unfolds as Danni enlists the help of the hunky new friend she has made named Joe. A romance develops between them, but does Joe know more about the murder and disappearance than he is letting on? Will Danni live to solve the murder?

Other titles available from G.W. Mullins include:

Timeless - An Adult Paranormal Romance Novel

The Native American Story Book Volume 1-5-
Stories Of The American Indians For Children

Walking With Spirits Volumes 1-6 Native American
Myths, Legends, And Folklore

The Native American Cookbook

Star People, Sky Gods And Other Tales of The
Native American Indians

Cherokee A Collection of American Indian Legends,
Stories And Fables

**Included at the end of this book, are the first two
chapters of G.W. Mullins' Best-Selling title
Rise Of The Dark Lighter Book One –
Dark Awakening**

For Clarence

Deep into that darkness peering, long I stood there, wondering, fearing, doubting, dreaming dreams no mortal ever dared to dream before.

Edgar Allan Poe

Before

The morning came quickly, as the three prepared to orb to the complex. As they closed in to stand together, Jen stood in the front, as Daniel and Zach stood behind her forming a pyramid shape.

Jen reached her arms behind, as they all took hands. She formed a shield around them as she focused her energy. Daniel followed behind with his addition of power. Jen looked over, and smiled at Zach, "Now it's your turn. Let the sand fly."

Zach had sand in his right hand waiting for the call. As he threw it upwards, the whole area that was filled with light, took on a golden tone. Jen increased her energy as she yelled, "Hold on."

The light lifted them into the air as a wormhole formed around them and they were sucked inside. The three held tight to each other as they were bounced around the shimmering passage. "Daniel, what's wrong with this orb, we are becoming unstable." Jen screamed, over the rumbling of the light walls around them.

"Just hold it together, we will make it. I think it is just because there is more mass than usual." He answered.

Jen watched, as she guided them to the end of the trip. She could see the opening in her mind as they slammed their way along. As the hall came closer, Jen could no longer hold on, and the protective shield disintegrated as they crashed into the wall of the hallway.

Jen rolled hard into a wall slamming her shoulder. Daniel managed to extend an energy wall in the last seconds to stop Zach and himself from crashing into each other. It was not a perfect landing, but they did survive the journey.

"Is everyone OK?" Daniel called out as they scrambled to their feet.

"Yes, I think." Zach called back.

"I think I might need a little help." Jen said as she struggled to get to her feet.

"Jen! You dislocated your shoulder." Daniel said as he ran over and put his hand over the area and it started to turn yellow. "How does that feel?" He asked.

"It hurts like a bitch, but I have had worse things done to me. Now, tell me, why did the orb break up like that?"

"I am beginning to think this place was protected by a shield or something. Doesn't matter now, we made it and we are all alive."

"Why is this place so quiet. I thought it would be like a factory?" Zach asked.

"You are right, it was noisy before. Something is different. Did we orb to the wrong place?" Jen said as she looked around. "No, this is the same place. There is the red sand." She said as she pointed towards the large vats that were filled to the top.

"Where did they all go? Are they invading already?" Zach asked.

"No, if they were, the vats would be emptied." Daniel turned to Jen and made a face. "Can you get anything from touching one of their personal objects?"

"Yeah, I can, now that I can move my arm again." She said as she moved to a table where one of the Sandmen had left his goggles.

Jen grasped them in her hands and pulled the red lenses closer. The memories of the owner flew forward, like she was driving down a highway. She pushed away useless memories and ones she did not want to see. And then, she saw the man put down his goggles as he prepared to leave for the queen's coronation.

"Their new queen is taking her crown today. I think we need to see this for ourselves." Jen insisted.

"Why would we want to see that?' Daniel asked "…and even if we did, how would we get in unseen."

Jen reached over to the wall where several uniforms hung. "Pick your size."

A short time after they were dressed, they followed the sound of the crowd outside moving down the hillside to the coronation gathering. Making their way through the crowd they came to the side of the elevated platform. It was there they saw Lacey, out of uniform and looking more like a queen's daughter. She did not notice them as they climbed the steps to get a better view.

The queen approached and prepared to receive her crown. She was covered in a sequined gown, and a veil that covered her face. She walked slowly and gracefully as she climbed one step at a time until she reached her throne.

As she turned to be seated, her daughter reached over to remove the veil, to show her face. The material fell softly from her skin, as she lit up with a smile and looked around to her gathered crowd. As she turned towards the three companions, Zach's stomach turned, as he felt as if he would throw up. He grabbed hard to Jen's hand as he stepped forward onto the stage and uttered one single word. "Mother!"

Chapter One

When Demons Attack

Jen looked up, just as she felt a wave of sand coating her face. She turned away as she started to orb, and the sensation of her body dematerializing began. She knew she had to escape, but to where? As the light of her orb flashed around her, she looked to Daniel who had grabbed ahold of Zach's arm, as they also began to orb.

The bright light of Jen's departure faded, and for a moment she felt relieved in her escape. The feeling did not last for long, as she emerged from her journey in a state of confusion. She had never chosen a destination, and she did not know where she was.

Around her was a building that looked familiar. She had been there before, and the memory chilled her to the bone. Her heart stopped as she remembered the Black Hat Man, better known as the demon Abraxas. Her hands trembled as she realized where she was. It was happening again, she had to escape before he attacked.

Jen scanned the directional signs as she walked through the building. Taking a deep breath, she headed for the elevator. As the doors closed, Jen felt claustrophobic, and as the confining box began to move, her stomach sank. The first few floors went quickly, and she felt a little relieved. Then the elevator stopped for no apparent reason.

Jen looked around, and time seemed to stop, like someone hit a pause button. She spun around and screamed, "Ok, who is playing games here?" She waited, and then nothing but silence. As she maneuvered her way to the control panel in front of her, Jen hit the emergency button. Nothing happened.

As she turned to the back of the elevator, she felt a sudden jerk. Then the floor felt like it was bouncing. Jen panicked as the elevator plummeted. She screamed for help, as her body was thrown upwards. The elevator fell floor after floor until reaching the basement where she was thrown to the floor.

As the doors opened, Jen jumped up and ran out into the hall. The remains of the destroyed innards of the elevator disappeared from view as the doors closed and the sign lit up showing movement towards the next floor. Jen turned and looked around her at the darkened basement she had been forced into.

She searched for the stairs but could not see any doors. Her mind raced frantically, not believing this could be happening again. She repeatedly said to herself that this was not real and it was a dream. Still, it did not erase her fear. In her mind, this was happening,

As she moved down the hall in front of her, the lights dimmed, and then began to flicker out to blackness, one by one. In the end, there was just one light left. Jen stopped moving and stood in one spot, as her nerves made her knees shake. She didn't know what to do.

"So nice of you to visit me again." A voice came from behind her.

She spun around to see the dark figure of a man approaching. "What do you want?"

"Well…you of course. To be specific, your spirit." The Black Hat Man laughed.

"Since I am not going to give it freely, I think you have a problem with that one."

"Oh, that is a problem we could remedy very quickly. Maybe then, your boyfriend would reveal himself."

"Sorry, I can't help you with that one, he isn't around right now." She said truthfully.

"Pity, but maybe, you would do, for the time being. One spirit is better than none." He laughed.

Jen looked down to the ring on her hand. It was emitting a glow. The brilliant blue stone seemed to be charged with power. Jen held it up, to look at it, and the light coming from the stone seemed to radiate. "Maybe I have a little help after all." Jen balled her fist together and aimed the ring in front of her. As the Black Hat man approached, she focused her mind on what she wanted, and the ring's glow got brighter.

As the Black Hat Man stepped within feet of her, the ring filled the room with its blue light. The intensity of the light blinded the man, and gave Jen her chance to find a way out. She scanned the hallway and doors until she found what she needed. The stairs were there all along, just invisible in the darkness. Jen ran for the door, but not before the Black Hat Man threw his leg out tripping her. As Jen fell to the ground, he grabbed her arm and held tight.

"You know, I grew up in a house with brothers, and one thing I learned early, was the one place a guy doesn't like to be kicked. Sorry about this, but I am not going down so easily." With the last of her words Jen kicked at the man. He doubled over in pain. Trying to move, he could not stand up, as Jen ran for the door to the stairs. All he could do is scream out to her, "You will pay for that, mark my words."

Jen climbed the stairs as fast as she could, arriving at the first floor. As she emerged from the doorway, the security guard turned to her. "Are you Ok Miss?" He asked. "Yes, I am fine. Never better." Jen smiled a nervous smile as she made her way into the hall. "I wouldn't suggest the elevator. We are having some problems." Jen just smiled. "I don't mind taking the stairs." A thought that resounded in her head as she turned a corner where no one could see as she surrounded herself with light and called out to Daniel.

Mullins

Chapter Two

The Land of Lost Things

Jen's head shook back and forth as she felt something touching her. She struggled to open her eyes, but the more she tried, the more she felt as if something was coating her face. Her mind raced as she came to the realization, she had been captured by a sandman.

The feeling she thought, had to be sand being poured over her. She was being induced into a dream state. She had not been with Abraxas; it was a memory pulled to the surface by the sandman. The power of the sand was holding her captive. She was a prisoner.

Jen struggled against the power the sandman had over her. She forced one eye open wide enough to see Daniel and Zach, who were propped up within reach of her. They were both stuck in their own forced dreams. Daniel jerked as his dream dominated him. Jen knew she had to get them out of there. If she could touch them, she could drag them with her as she orbed away.

Jen breathed deeply as the sand man turned in the other direction. It was then or never, she thought to herself. Struggling to control her body, Jen reached forward and grabbed hold of her friends.

Her mind filled with a fear that made her tremble, but also fueled her inner power. As she drew on the power to form a shield and initiated an orb, her eyes flew open. She felt the power, surge forward. She was back in control, but the feeling changed as the energy she emitted surrounded all three of them.

Jen looked on in amazement as her shield color changed to black. She took a deep breath and cleared her mind as she chose a destination in her mind. The Sandman turned as he saw the unusual flash of blackness fill the area. As he turned to grab

Jen, it was too late, the flash of light drug them into nothingness.

Jen felt the change from within her, as their bodies changed into a form of energy. As they traveled through the wormhole of light, something came over Jen. She was no longer the same, she was changing. She was no longer in control. It was as if some other lifeform was inhabiting her.

Jen screamed out in fear, as she felt herself being drug through the energy bridge. She called for Daniel who was still unconscious. There was no one who could save her now. She struggled to gain control as she searched for a destination to end their orb. One opening came up in the distance, the Land of Lost Things. She had no choice, she had to free herself from the power.

As they flew out of the end of the orb, Jen let go of the others and they flew in different directions. Soaring from the sky, Jen flew towards the ground and bounced into the sand dune below her. She hit hard, and the sand was no comfort, as it burnt her skin as she tried to reach out to steady herself.

Jen tried to catch her breath as she struggled in the sand, to get upright. With every motion her feet slid to one side or the other. Her anger raged, as she felt the energy lifeforce struggling to get ahold of her again. She screamed out, "No!" as the power pulled her upwards into the sky.

As she looked upwards to open her eyes, the force took her over. A darkness covered her vision. Where she once had beautiful hazel eyes, now there was a glowing blackness. Her arms flew outwards to her sides and her body glowed as energy was emerging from her skin.

"I am free. Now and forever, I am a goddess. No one will ever control me again." Jen's voice grew deeper and more sinister. A smile crossed her lips, whatever was in control of her now, had no plans of letting go.

Inside, Jen watched in horror, as she had no control over her own body. She had no idea how to fight back. Her energy had no effect over what was happening. She was a prisoner in her own body. Jen reached out to Daniel, if he was in any control, he would be able to hear her message. As she projected, three words got through, before the entity stopped her, "Please help me."

Chapter Three

Daniel Returns to the Land of the Dead

As Daniel fell from the sky, his body spun around. He had no idea of what was happening to him. The sand that coated him and robbed him of his consciousness, held him in a dream of his past. He was helpless until the dream had run its course.

~~~~~

As Daniel stumbled into his first steps, he looked around in fear. He did not know where he was, or why he was there. When he first focused his eyes, the cemetery looked for the most part empty. That illusion changed quickly.

As his sight adjusted; he was able to see things he had never seen before. For the first time in
~~~~~

his young life, he saw the dead. As they converged in on him, he quickly realized he was not alone. Stepping back in fear, he scanned the group of spirits moving towards him. His mind raced for a way to escape.

There were so many of them coming at him at once. The ghosts appeared from all different time periods. Some of them looked to be over a hundred years old. Some were dressed in elegant dresses made of lace and embroidery, and some had expensive suits. Others were more modest and seemed to be of different groups. Some looked as normal as a person you just walked past on the street, and others looked as if they had died violent deaths. Their distorted images were covered in blood or mutilation. Those were the ones that scared Daniel the most.

The group drew in, and surrounded him, before Daniel could escape. Their voices rang out in a mixed mess that was unintelligible. Daniel pulled back from them, trying to make sense of what any of them were saying. So many of them asked questions, and shouted at him wanting to know about the outside world. Some of them looked distraught, asking if their families were ok, or still alive. Daniel being in his confused state, was terrified, he didn't know what to do. His first thought, was to escape any way he could.

As Daniel closed his eyes, in his mind he visualized a place where none of these spirits or walking dead were near him. The more he desired his freedom, the more he felt a strange power spinning deep within. This feeling had never been there before, it was raw and unbridled.

He felt himself panic, as the feeling grew stronger. As he looked down at his hands, he saw the blueish glow begin. Suddenly a blue shaft of light formed around him, and his body began to become more transparent. As the shaft of light engulfed him, Daniel faded from where he was. It took only seconds, for him to disappear from where he was standing and reappear over fifty feet from the crowd.

Daniel looked around, not sure how he had gotten away. How could he have made this happen? He then knew, things would never be the same again. Being he was in the cemetery, gave him all the answers he needed. He had never been able to do such things as a human, but as a spirit, maybe things were different. He wasn't prepared to be dead, especially so early in life. He had just turned seventeen in the hospital as he lay in a coma. His death was a peaceful one, but it left him with so many questions.

As the crowd looked around, they located Daniel, and started to move in his direction again. His mind flashed to the zombie movies he had seen at the local theater. He was not ready to be one of the living dead. He looked around to find some safe place to run. All he saw were tombstones, and a few mausoleums. He didn't know how to hide from the dead.

"Come with me, if you want to get away from them." A voice came from behind him.

Daniel jumped in fear, as he turned to face the voice. "Ok, if it gets me away from them."

As Daniel ran behind, he studied the girl who had come to his rescue. She looked very much out of place for his time period. Daniel was born in 1950 and died in 1967. He was the typical white bread boy jock and socialite. This girl was different, she wore tattered clothes from a hundred years before him. Her hair and look, were not of a typical girl of his time. She looked like a servant, no, he thought, maybe worse, a slave. He just couldn't place the look. For the moment it did not matter.

As they hid in a secluded spot, the crowd passed them by. They were safe for the moment. At least, as safe as someone running from an army of the dead. Daniel studied the girl who had saved him. He looked her up and down, trying to make sense of who she was, and why she helped him.

"Why are you staring at me? You never seen a colored girl before?" She asked.

"I'm sorry, I don't mean to be rude. Just, everyone here seems to be from a different time period. I was trying to figure out where you were from."

"Fair enough…I am Abigail Washington. I was born in 1850, on a plantation in Virginia. I died on my 19th birthday. Killed by the master of the house, as I was escaping with my mother. My mama was more lucky than me, she got away. She brought me here, and buried me on the outskirts of the cemetery where no one would see. Now, you know who I am. As for that crowd chasing you, they are just as dead as we are. They don't really mean harm; they are just scared. Most of them do not realize how long they have been here. When a new spirit shows up, they think there is some hope for communication or something. They're just trying to make sense of this is all. They ought to now, there ain't no sense in death. Now, head into this building, we will be safe in here."

"Abigail, why are there so many ghosts roaming this place?" Daniel asked.

"Some don't know how to leave. They got no other place to go. They stay, hoping the light will come and find them, but it don't. It's just like that sometimes. Don't do any good to try to understand it. The light didn't come for me, and I have been here a long time." Abigail said lowering her head.

"I was always told; you pass over when you die." Daniel tried to look her in the eye as he spoke, but Abigail always looked down.

"If you are a churchgoer, they tell you all that. Don't know if it is true or not. Some of these people just got unfinished things to do, I guess. It's just how it works. Maybe one day, we'll all be free, but 'til then we stuck in the boneyard." She tried to laugh and find humor in their situation.

"Why did they all have to attack me like that?" he asked.

"Cause, they are scared and want to know about their families. Most of them don't even know how long they have been here. The days just mix together, when you are dead. Not like we got much to do, but roam." Abigail smiled, as she looked into Daniel's eyes for the first time. "You got pretty blue eyes. I like blue, it's my favorite color."

"Thank you. And thanks for saving me like you did."

"I didn't save you…you saved yourself, when you orbed away from them. You could have lost them if you wanted to."

"Maybe, if I had known what I was doing. I don't know any of this dead spirit existence. What does orbed mean?" Daniel was confused about all of it.

"When you made that light form around you, and then you moved from place to place. That is how you orb."

"You mean, I did that on purpose."

"Yup, and you can do a lot more things, if you set your mind to it. You just gonna have to want-to first, and then it will come to you." Abigail laughed at Daniel, because he looked like a child with a new toy.

"I didn't know what I was doing, it just happened. I don't even know how to do it again. Can everyone do this?" he asked.

"Nope, not everyone, just them ones who have the gift. You don't see it every day. It was your light that attracted them to you, when you showed up. You looked like a god to them, a chosen one."

"Chosen by who, and to do what?" Daniel cocked his head not understanding.

"Who knows? But I will be here if you need me. You just need to calm down, and not be so scared of the dead. You know you are dead, right?" Abigail laughed out very loud.

"Yeah, I got that part already." Daniel smiled.

"How'd you die?"

Daniel looked down for a second, and then back to Abigail. He shook his head from side to side. "I was sure I knew, when I got here. Now, I am not so sure anymore. My head really hurts. Maybe it was something to do with that."

"It's ok, sometimes people get confused in the beginning. Maybe you got something to work out."

"Unfinished business…that's all I need. Can we leave the cemetery?" He asked.

"No, we're stuck here. I tried to leave once, and as soon as I grabbed the front gate, it sent a charge through me so hard, I was thrown back across the cemetery. I won't be trying that again anytime soon."

"So, we are stuck here waiting for the light, which may never come, and a chance to go to the other side, we may never get."

"That's about the half of it." Abigail laughed.

"Well at least I have a friend to talk to." Daniel smiled at her.

As Daniel and Abigail said their last words, the light outside the window seemed to fade. They looked out onto the cemetery, and there seemed to be a black fog rolling across the ground. Abigail opened the door, as she stepped out, a look of confusion crossed her face. She had never seen this before, not in the hundred years she had been there. She turned to Daniel, "Ain't no good gonna come from this."

Mullins

Chapter Four

Something Evil This Way Comes

As Daniel walked out of the doorway, he was sure Abigail was right, nothing good was coming, the dark was awakening. On the hill just in front of him, a dark void swirled. He studied it hard as he looked into the center of the darkness. He was sure there was a shape deep within it.

Daniel felt a chill in the air that filled his lungs. He trembled for a second as he studied the form that emerged. He could not make out the features of the shape, but it was a woman, of that much, he was sure. His senses drew him to the form. She was familiar, and his urges told him to go to her.

Daniel wiped his eyes and turned away. He remembered this place and this memory. He lived this before, just after he died, but this was not the ending he experienced. In his memory, this is where the Dark-Lighter first showed himself. He remembered Malachi, and their first battle. Daniel nearly destroyed the cemetery. It was a memory hidden from him for so long by the Guardians.

He shook his head; this was not right. As his head began to hurt from the cloudiness that felt like he was drugged, he knew he was being controlled. It was a Sandman. When they found the Queen, his memory became clouded. He had to have been forced into Dreamworld, but why change the end of his memory.

Daniel turned back to the woman emerging from the void. As she moved forward, her features took shape. She looked at Daniel as he fell to his knees. He knew her, it was Jen, just not like he had ever seen her. There was a sinister quality to her now. She had been changed, and Daniel sensed it.

After Jen died at the hands of the demon Abraxas, she ascended and was given her life back as a White-Lighter. As she developed her abilities and power, she and Daniel shared a rapport. They seemed to know when the other was in danger or needed help. They formed a connection that stretched over time and space. The only time this rapport did not work, was in Dreamland after Jen had disappeared and Daniel came for her.

Daniel sat back on his heels and looked up to the woman, as he focused his power to scan her mind. He needed to know if she was real. As he delved deeper into her mind, he saw Jen. Deep inside, she was a captive to who or whatever had control of her body.

Daniel flew backwards as he stood up. Whatever this was, she was evil and darkness surrounded her. If he was to win Jen back, it could not happen here in a dream state, he had to escape the memory.

He ran backwards for a short distance and then called out to her. "I don't know why you came here. I don't even know what you want. I am assuming since you have claimed Jen's body, you are here to take me." He gasped for air as he stood staring. "I promise you; I will not give in so easily. I am leaving this memory now."

Daniel looked over to Abigail and smiled. "It was so good to see you again. I had forgotten how much I really missed you." With his final words, he summoned all the power he had within, and formed a blue orb around himself. The only destination he could think of was wherever Zach was. Perhaps there would be safety in numbers.

Daniel's blue light filled the area, as he lifted from the ground and spun around. In seconds his form disappeared and he transported to Zach. He rejoined his body which lay on the ground. Struggling, he shook off the effects of the sand and blinked his eyes open.

He gasped for air, as he sat up and reached for Zach's arm. Daniel pulled at him, trying to awaken him from the dream state. Nothing seemed to work, and then Daniel raised a hand above his head and emitted a yellow healing light.

Zach jerked violently, until he was able to open his eyes and see Daniel. "Ok, I am back, thanks to you." Zach ran a hand to his head and rubbed his eyes. The pain of being ripped from the sand, filled his head. He hurt in a way that felt like a ball bat had just hit his head. "Oh Daniel, this hurt is something I wouldn't wish on anyone."

"I know." Daniel replied. "Get ready, it is about to get so much worse."

"What do you mean?" Zach looked at him hard, trying to understand what was happening.

"Just behind me when I orbed, was a being of immense energy. She is evil and inhabiting Jen's body. She's coming for me."

Back on the cemetery hilltop, the entity moved towards Abigail. She studied her as she moved closer, step by step. A crooked smile crossed her face, as she scanned through Jen's memories. She searched until she found what she was looking for. Deep within her past, Jen had buried her time with Abigail. She loved her so much, and Abigail's death was too painful.

As the creature stopped directly in front of her, Abigail looked straight into her eyes. "What do you want here?" She asked in a trembling voice.

"Nothing, nothing at all." The morphed demonic voice came from within.

"Daniel is gone now; you cannot hurt him." Abigail insisted.

"It's not him I am trying to hurt." She said as the coldness of her voice filled the air.

As the words drifted away, Jen knew it was all about her. The entity knew she could see what was happening. This was a ploy to weaken her and keep control. Jen wasn't about to let that happen, but the entity was a quick study, and had hit Jen in a wound, that was still sore to that day.

Jen slammed back against the entity in an attempt to show she was still in the fight. She seized control for a moment and turned to Abigail, "I know you are a memory, but I do miss you." Jen turned to walk away.

"Do I know you?" Abagail asked.

"Not at this point in time, but in your future, we became sisters. Farewell."

Jen felt her power dwindling as the entity forced its way to control again. As it searched for the orb trail Daniel had left behind, the dark swirl of black energy filled the air and enveloped her body, before disappearing into nothing.

Mullins

Chapter Five

Child of Darkness

"Where the hell are we?" Daniel asked.

"For lack of a better name, I would call it 'The Land of Lost Things' or something like that." Zach said laughing.

As they cleared their heads and looked around, they were both aware the name fit. The ground, for as far as the eye could see, was covered with sand similar to a desert. Thrown all around, in every direction, were items from the earth's history. This strange place seemed to be a repository for lost people, places and things.

Daniel reached out a hand to pull Zach to his feet, before venturing forward into the landscape. As they walked, they passed objects from different time periods. Many things looked as new as the day they had been lost. There had been no aging here, or degradation.

Daniel stopped short, as he looked to the side where a squadron of naval jet fighters were parked side by side. Walking up to touch one, he studied it, and the rest, to reassure himself they were real. As he ran his fingers across the insignia of the plane, he knew he was right.

"I know these." Daniel said as he got excited.

"What do you mean you know these?" Zach looked at him confused.

"These planes are a part of history. They disappeared in World War 2."

"No way. These planes are practically new. They could only be a couple of years old." Zach insisted.

"No, they were a couple of years old, when they were lost back on December 5, 1945. There were 5 planes off the coast of Florida. They disappeared over the Bermuda Triangle, after losing contact during a United States Navy overwater navigation training flight from Naval Air Station Fort Lauderdale." Daniel said smiling as he held onto the plane.

"…And how do you know this?" Zach asked.

"I love planes and things missing from history. I just wonder how they got here. Seems weird this other universe is catching all these things from earth." Daniel's voice trailed off. "Maybe it is not so weird. I mean, we got here through orbing, which is transporting from one place to another. Maybe back on earth there are doorways where things fall through like wormholes. Maybe the Bermuda Triangle is one of those places."

"You are crazy. Then again, it would explain all the ships and planes around here. Hmmm, if I stay here much longer, I will go crazy." Zach tried to keep himself from being overwhelmed, as he stared out over the massive landscape of things deposited there."

"If these planes are here, and the ships and other things, …where are the people who came here with them?" Daniel wondered.

"They would have to be here somewhere. They obviously did not die in their planes or ships. There are no bodies." Zach scanned the area, but saw no one.

They began to walk towards the skyline, and along the way they stopped and explored everything from pyramids to a lost city of the Ancients. Each and everything they saw, looked as it was intact and still as the day it arrived.

"Daniel, were we deliberately placed here, like a prison?" Zach asked.

"I have no idea, but if this is a prison, it is a hell of an amazing place to be trapped.

Just as Daniel stopped speaking, he heard a sound coming from the distance. It started out low and then began to get louder. Something was coming their way. Daniel spun around and saw the bright silver plane reflecting in the sun, as it flew towards him. He stared hard as it shot overhead. "I know that one, it is a twin-engine Lockheed 10E Electra." Daniel screamed.

"Of course, it is. You are too into history man."

Yes, I am. I was born a long time ago and you would not understand. I was before the time of internet. Back in my day, people read books and learned things." Daniel laughed.

"And when were you born." Zach asked.

"I was born in 1950. I died in 1967. Then I came back to life a few years ago."

"Wait, you are like over 70 years old." Zach froze, not being able to conceive the idea.

"Look, I spent almost 60 years in a cemetery waiting for someone to hear me. Then Jen came along, and I was freed. Shortly afterwards, I was given a chance at life in a new way. Now, I am more than human."

"You are an Angel." Zach said smiling.

"Angel, White-Lighter, whatever you call it, I am here and alive, so to speak. And for that, I am grateful for a second chance. I know I am not like you; I have had a lot of years to be different and study life."

"I think you are pretty cool, for an old man."

In the sky above them, the airplane circled as if someone was studying them. Daniel waved to the pilot, as it searched for a place to land. With all of the lost items thrown all about, landing was not an easy task.

As the plane found a clearing near them, it touched down, throwing sand into the air all around them. Daniel ran to the plane in excitement, to see it up close. As he stopped and Zach caught up to him, the door to the plane opened.

Through the opening, the pilot's head appeared. She was a rather tall thin woman. Her wavy brown hair moved back and forth in the breeze as she jumped down to the ground. "Hello boys. Am I glad to see you." The pilot yelled out.

Daniel staired at her, studying her face, he began to smile. "I know you." He blurted out.

"I don't know how, son, I have been here for a really long time. I don't recall meeting you." She replied.

"No, not from here. Back on earth. You are Amelia, aren't you?" He said getting excited.

"Yes, I am. But how did you know that?"

"Daniel, how do you know her? She has to be from the 1930's." Zach asked.

"1939 to be exact, don't you get it? She is Amelia Earhart!" Daniel screamed.

"No way. Unless she came here as you said."

"Fellas, I don't mean to interrupt your excitement. I mean, I am flattered that you remember me. But I think we have another bigger problem to deal with."

"Like what?" Daniel asked.

"Like that big black bird in the sky, that looks like a big ball of energy coming right at us." Amelia said pointing to the sky.

As the bird came closer, the energy emitted from it made a loud screeching noise. Like a Phoenix from the flames, this bird's wings filled the sky flapping back and forth. It was coming for them, and there was no stopping it.

Chapter Six

Like a Phoenix

Daniel looked upwards at the large darkened energy mass, that blocked the light in its direction. He called out to Jen in his mind, desperately trying to make contact, but there was no reply. He was sure Jen was still alive within this creature that had taken control of her body.

As the creature descended, Daniel studied it. He was not a weak man; he was an angel after all. His greatest fear would be hurting Jen. As the creature hovered above them, with its huge birdlike form flapping its wings, people came forward from their hiding places.

Amelia turned to look behind her at the mass of people that was developing. "Uh, guys, I think we have company." She spoke. "Maybe we need to figure out what is going on, before this gets out of control." As she walked up to Daniel and placed a hand on his shoulder. "Look, you seem like a terrific young man, and I get the feeling you are holding a lot back because you know that thing, ...whatever it is. I am not an expert on a lot of things, but I do know if you wait too long, sometimes you lose the advantage."

"I know, and I appreciate the advice. I was just hoping it would not come to this." Daniel hung his head. "I don't want to hurt her."

Daniel felt a pain in his chest, as he breathed in and blew it out. He looked to Amelia and smiled. She knew he was thanking her for giving him a bit of courage. "Zach, do whatever you can to control them." Zach shook his head and headed towards the crowd.

Daniel walked a short distance, and with every step, he watched the entity. It was waiting for him to make a move. He was also waiting for himself to do something. He closed his eyes for a moment and gathered his energy from within. As his eyes opened, he formed a blue colored shield around himself, and as he lifted from the ground, his wings took shape.

He never used his wings much, and in most situations, he felt them unnecessary. In this situation, if the entity was presenting itself as a goddess, then he would become godlike. As he flapped his wings and lifted higher into the sky, the large crowd below gathered together and watched.

Daniel looked straight forward at the entity as he came close enough to speak. "What do you want? Why are you following me?" Daniel asked.

"Well, I want you, of course." The dark staticky voice echoed from Jen's body.

"Sorry, but I am taken, and as soon as I get you out of her body, Jen and I, will be together again,"

"That's easier said than done. You see, I like it in here. Experiencing life as a human is so much more exciting than I ever imagined it to be." The entity said smugly.

"You cannot just take another's body. Jen has a life she is entitled to."

"I like experiencing human traits like emotions and excitement. I am not going anywhere." She snapped back at him.

"That's fine, you see, you may be a being of darkness, but I am a child of light. The light always wins." Daniel smiled at her as he pulled from the deep well of energy within him.

Sensing his eminent attack, the entity stretched her arms out wide, and cast a shade all around the land below. The area quickly became a dark void and the innocent bystanders were about to be pulled into it.

Daniel looked on, as the darkness formed into a sort of black hole. Winds whipped in the direction of the darkness, as their force increased. Sand began to blow and turned into a storm that carried smaller debris with it. Daniel knew he had to stop this now, before anyone was hurt.

As he flung his arms outwards, his wings flapped forcefully and his light force grew outwardly. Daniel was determined, he could not back down. As he forced his energy forward, the entity turned her attention away from the dark void and back to him. She was ready to fight.

As her head flew backwards, the head of the great black bird turned upwards releasing a thunderous war cry. The ground shook as the bird sent out wave after wave of blasting sound. The entity took satisfaction in the fear she was inflicting on the crowd. And then there was Daniel, she did not understand why he would not back away in fear.

"Leave them alone. If it is me you want, then let's do this." Daniel challenged her.

The entity drew closer, to within arm's reach of him. Her head lifted up and Daniel looked into her eyes. Then he felt it for a brief moment. It was Jen, she was fighting for control.

Daniel called out to her. "Jen if you can hear me, please fight. Help me to defeat her."

"Daniel!" Jen's voice came from within the creature. "I don't know how to, or what to do. She is so strong. You have to attack."

"No, I won't hurt you. There has to be another way." He pleaded with her.

"There is nothing else you can do. If you and the others are to survive, then you have to kill me. Please, do it now, while I have control. There is no other way." Jen's voice trailed off as she struggled to hold on. "Now, Daniel!"

Daniel took hold of his power and channeled it forward towards the entity. As he filled the air with his blueish light, the entity struggled, and her black energy bird, threw its wings backwards and forwards violently attempting to maintain itself.

The entity fell backwards as Daniel charged toward it. A tear ran down the side of his face as he struggled with the task he had been challenged with.

As the creature fell to the ground, the energy bird dissipated.

Daniel landed just steps from her feet, and looked onward, as he continued to wrap her in his energy. As he looked down, he saw the pain in her face. He felt Jen within the entity, she was suffering. Her pain was unimaginable.

Daniel's breathing increased, as he screamed out in pain. Jen's rapport with him was channeling all that she was feeling. Daniel drew back from his attack, knowing the woman he loved was about to die. It was in that moment of weakness, the entity took control of the battle, and lifted upwards to the sky.

As she climbed higher, she turned to him. "You are very powerful, but I have the trump card. As long as you cannot hurt her, I will always win. I will be back for you."

Chapter Seven

The Lost One

Zach watched as the entity flew away and disappeared from his sight. He walked to Daniel's side, just as he fell to the ground. His power had been withdrawn; he did not fall from weakness. He fell to the ground from the pain inside him. He loved Jen more than anyone he had ever known. The pain was too much.

"Are you OK?" Zach said looking down at him.

"No…I don't think I am. I couldn't do it. I had the power to destroy this creature and I could not hurt Jen to do so." Daniel doubled over trying to speak.

"And that says more about you than anything I could ever learn from getting to know you."

Amelia spoke as she came up from behind. "That is pure love, and you are capable of so many things, but not hurting someone. It is how it should be."

"We have to stop her; she will destroy everything here. Everyone will die." Zach added.

"You don't know that." Amelia challenged him.

"No, he is right. I have abilities. More than you saw here, and I can see things that might happen. This creature is a destroyer of worlds. She is out of control evil. I didn't know it, until I was overpowering her in the end. She does not have a moral counter that tells her when to stop."

"Then what do we do?" Zach asked.

"We work together, and when she comes back, we do what we have to do, to take her out." Daniel replied.

"Can you do that? Can you kill and innocent to save the lives of others?" Amelia asked.

"I don't think I have a choice."

"Then, let's get prepared. We don't know how long we have." Zach said, holding out a hand to Daniel.

"Did anyone speak with these people? Do we know where we are?" Daniel asked.

"I did, and apparently this place is what we thought it to be, a Land of Lost Things. Apparently, this is a pocket universe used by the Sandmen. They have portals all over the earth, and when things disappear, as they always do, they end up here. Ever lose a sock? It is probably here." Amelia explained.

"So, all the disappearances of ships, boats and people…they are all here?" Daniel asked.

"Yes, and it gets better. No one here seems to age. Not even the ships or planes, they stay in the same state as when they arrived. It is as if time stands still. The area just keeps getting populated by new arrivals."

"Yeah, and no departures." Zach added.

"We will find a way out. Just might take a minute." Daniel tried to calm him.

"Do I have to remind you, of the Sandman war about to begin against the people of earth? They do not stand a chance if we do not get out."

"Point taken."

As Daniel walked towards the growing crowd of people, he studied them. There were people from all stages of history. It would seem the Sandman portals were active for over 100 years.

He studied their faces and how they all looked healthy and frozen in time. He wished he could send them home, but there was no way to send them back in time to their families. So many of them would be gone now. He was reminded of his time in the cemetery, so many spirits from different times. So many wanting to go back to their families that had been dead for so long.

Daniel shook his head. He did not know how to fix this situation, or if he should. As he walked amongst the crowd, they all turned to him. Looking on, like he was some sort of savior, they waited for him to speak.

"Well, go on." A voice rose from the crowd.

Daniel looked out awkwardly, he did not know what to say. As he looked around, he knew he had to do something. Clinching his fists together, he mustered the energy to levitate himself upwards, so all could see him.

"Hello everyone. At first when we came, we thought no one else was here. Boy, were we wrong, there are so many of you. You guys seem to be looking to me for answers. I can't say I have any yet. All I can say is, we will be prepared when the entity returns and we will fight. And if we win that fight, then we will band together to find a way out of here. I just want you to understand, I am not all powerful. I do have abilities, but then again, we all have talents, and working together, just might save us all." Daniel slowly drifted to the ground as the crowd watched and seemed to believe in what he said.

As Zach and Amelia escorted him back towards her plane, Daniel spoke. "Do you think they believed me?"

"I'd bet money on it." Amelia said laughing.

"I just did not want to come across as some fake messiah." Daniel whispered.

"Naw, you did good kid." She said slapping him on the back.

"Now we just need to worry about the entity." Zach added

Just out of sight of the people, the entity found a place of seclusion. She landed on the ground preparing to heal.

"He won't stop until he has defeated you." Jen poked at her.

"Don't you ever shut up?" The entity screamed.

"Does it annoy you when I speak? Maybe the truth hurts. It's cool, I have nothing else to do but talk ...all day and all night."

"If I could come inside and destroy you, I would."

"Anytime Bitch, I am ready and waiting." Jen prodded her.

The entity raised her hands and grabbed ahold of her head. She had been taken off guard by Daniel's attack, and with Jen's constant unrest, she could not focus on the peace she needed to heal. Her rage grew, as she planned her attack. She would have Daniel and his power. Even if it meant she had to kill him to absorb it.

Mullins

Chapter Eight

Relics

As Amelia guided Daniel back to the front of her plane, she watched as he looked up in amazement. As he staired up at the propellers, Amelia watched him with pride. She understood how much he appreciated what she loved so much.

"You really like it don't you?" Amelia asked as she smiled at him.

"Yes mam, I do. I was always a fan of yours back when I was little. Heck, even when I was a teenager. Up until I…." His words trailed off.

"Until what?" She asked.

"I am not sure you would understand. It is a situation that is hard to explain." Daniel answered.

"Try me. I am a pretty with-it kind of gal." She said laughing.

"Ok, you asked for it. Hmmm…I am dead. I died over seventy years ago. I am now what is called a White-Lighter, or you can say angel. I was sent back to be a sort of guardian or protector. The entity you saw is also an angel. She has been possessed by some entity. So, I have to free her, and along with Zach, we have to stop a pending invasion of earth by a group of beings known as the Sandmen."

Amelia walked away, and spun on the heel of her shoe and looked him in the face. "Yeah, that was more than I ever imagined. An angel, uh yeah, that is beyond imagination. So, if you and the girl are angels what is the boy, Zach?"

"He is a Sandman." He said smiling.

"Wait, you said they were invading the earth. Yet you have one with you.?"

"He is a good guy. He didn't even know he was a Sandman until recently. He wants to set things right."

"Well, I think I got it all. All I can say, is whatever you need, I will help. I just don't know what good I could be, with my plane stuck here in this place."

"How did you get here? I mean what happened when you left earth and landed here?" Daniel asked as he paced back and forth nervously.

"I don't really understand it. I was flying with Fred over the ocean and we were running low on fuel. I was looking for some place, any place to land. We just had nowhere to go. I tried to get Fred to help me figure it all out, but he was on the sauce. Just as I was about to give up, the plane started to go down. And as we were about to hit water, the bright light came up from underneath us. Man, it was big, and it surrounded the whole plane, and came up towards the sky, Then the sound of the ocean disappeared, and the light started to come from above, and we were over land. So, I landed."

"So where is Fred? If he came with you, what happened to him?" Daniel asked trying to be careful not to offend.

"He is here, passed out in the back of the plane. He went on a bender last night and I just left him there, I couldn't deal with his drunken butt anymore." She laughed out loud, knowing she was acting like an embattled wife of an alcoholic.

Just as she finished speaking, she heard a rumble within the plane. He was awake, and Amelia put her guard up for the hangover, that was about to become her problem. Fred stumbled to the door of the plane and looked around. He had no idea where he was, or what had just happened.

"Where are we? I thought we were on patrol." Fred questioned her.

"I had to land. There are new people here, who are trying to help us go home." She called back to him. "Just relax and let your head calm down.

"My dad used to warn me about alcohol. Now I see why." Daniel laughed.

"I bet your dad was proud. You seem to have turned out like a great kid."

"I guess he was. I died when I was 17. In a way that seems like such a short time in life."

Yeah, I guess so. All I know is, I just met you and I am glad to know you." She walked over and touched his shoulder in a motherly way. The sentiment was not wasted on Daniel.

Daniel raised his head and smiled at her just as his brain started registering what Fred had said. He looked at the plane and thought about how Amelia had flown overhead. There were so many questions flying through his head, he had to sort it out before he opened his mouth.

"You said, that you were low on fuel, the light took you, and landed your plane here. But how is it you were just flying.?"

"After we landed here, there were so many other planes and ships just sitting around loaded with fuel, hell, even fuel transports. We figured out ways to syphon fuel and transport it to my plane. There is enough to keep me flying for decades. There are those here that have helped. We formed a kind of collective community that looks out for each other. They appointed me as a surveyor in the air. I fly around for a couple of hours each day looking for new arrivals. Just like you." She smiled at him.

"How do you all survive here? What do you do for food and necessities?" He asked.

"You would be amazed how often the things we need, just arrive from the sky or just appear. We have never needed for anything. I was wondering for a long time, if someone was keeping us here and supplying what we needed."

"Could that be possible?" Daniel wondered.

"I don't know, but we are all well, and never without what we need."

"Amelia, if you came in to this place, who is to say there is not a way to go right back out."

"Sweetheart, if there is a way out, I have been looking for over eighty years and never found it."

"I am just saying, if you came through a door, why can't you go back out it?"

"Maybe it is just a door in. An entrance, with no exit." She tried to find her words.

"Point taken. I was just being hopeful that we could find an opening and fly right back out."

"Daniel, it should be so easy. But if there are openings all around here, who says they will go back to where we came from? I mean, we are all from different times. What if the openings are located in different times as well as different places? We could all go through and end up god knows where." She laughed at him as she opened her mouth again. "See, I am more than just a pretty face.

They both broke into laughter. Daniel looked at her rough chiseled features, studying her. She was more of a tomboy than your typical older woman. As he looked at her, he thought in her own way she was an attractive woman.

"Whatcha staring at?" She asked.

"Nothing much, you are just a pretty cool lady is all. I feel lucky to have met you. Just wish it was in a different situation where we weren't stuck fighting our way out."

"I feel the same way. But when we get out…and we will. I owe you a burger and milkshake. They still have those out there, right?"

"Yes, they do, and I will definitely take you up on the offer."

"For now though, can you take me up for a run around the area. I want to see what we have to work with." He asked.

"You got it kid. Climb aboard and I will give you the scenic tour."

The plane taxied around the open space, and the people moved back to give her room to take off. Zach sat on the wing of one of the Flight 19 planes and watched them leave. As he watched, he pulled at his sand pouch, removing from the side a knife, that was tucked in its holder. Lifting the knife into the light, he studied the insignia of the sandman. The light of the sun, reflected from the triangle, with its lines waving through.

Holding the knife in the air, he noticed the light projecting through, formed a shape on the wing of the plane. As he stared hard, he saw the image of a map taking shape. There had been a star map inside. He looked at it, and the landscape. It all made sense to him, This, could be a guide to the portals from earth to the Land of Lost Things.

Chapter Nine

Ghost Flight

Daniel climbed forward into the cockpit of the plane, as Fred left his seat. Amelia reached over and tapped as an invitation for Daniel to sit down. A smile crossed his face, as he realized he was about to achieve a childhood dream. As he sat down next to Amelia, she turned to him and smiled. "Betcha never thought you would ever get to be my co-pilot."

Looking out of the windows, the plane climbed higher and higher above the sand covered ground they had just left. Daniel sat back into his seat and studied the controls all around him. He was awestruck.

"Is it all you hoped it would be?" She asked him.

"All that, and more. Thank-you for this. I never thought I would live to see the day." He said as his voice grew quieter.

"What's up kid, is something wrong?"

"No, I just realized what I said. I guess I never did live to see." Daniel responded.

"Don't let it get to you. You are here, and you are living a boyhood dream. So, in a way, you did get what you wanted."

"Yeah, I guess so. Wow, there are so many things here. I guess for as long as the portals have been opened, this is right."

Amelia swung the plane to the left, and flew towards one of the suns. From the back of the plane Fred let out a scream. As the plane had turned, he had dropped his liquor bottle, and it crashed to the metal floor.

Amelia smiled as she looked over her shoulder. "That will teach you." She yelled out over the plane's engine rumble.

As they continued on their journey, Amelia looked forward in their path as a new plane headed their way. "Lock your straps, this might get a bit bumpy." Amelia dove under the oncoming plane which seemed to be aimed at her.

As she plunged her plane downward, Amelia flashed on her last time diving towards the ocean. Her mind raced, as she recalled the last messages that she called out for help. She said, "We are on the line 157-337 flying north and south. "We are on you but cannot see you." Then nothing but radio silence.

The plane rumbled and shook as Amelia was snapped out of her memory. Reaching for her radio, she called to the other plane. "Pull up before you get us all killed." The plane did not respond.

As she swung down and whipped around the other plane, she showed her experience as a pilot. Climbing back upwards, she matched the speed of the other plane. As they came along side, they could see through the windows. One by one, they looked in as they saw the passengers, who seemed to already be dead.

As they came to the front of the plane, Amelia could see the pilots were slumped over. She turned her head. There wasn't much they could do for them now. Amelia backed her plane off and tried to predict where the other plane would crash.

"They don't come here like that. I have never seen a plane of the dead come through a portal. Must mean they died by some unusual incident on the other side. For all of them to be dead, makes no sense. Unless they were hijacked."

Daniel stared at the plane, as Fred came to his side. "You alright kid?" He asked.

"Yeah, I am fine. It's just sad so many people dead at one time." Daniel answered.

"Let it go, there is nothing you can do to save the dead." Fred said in a gravelly voice.

As Daniel looked on, he saw movement on the plane. At first, he thought it was his eyes playing tricks on him. Then, he was sure. He looked hard over the distance. As he got a good view, he knew what he was seeing. When he was trapped in the cemetery, he had seen it so many times. The bodies were dead, but their spirits stilled screamed out for help. It was usually the result of a tragic death. They did not know yet that they were dead.

Daniel had helped cross over so many spirits like these before. It was part of what he was trained for. He felt saddened that he could not help them now. Even if the plane crashed, he would not be able to help them go into the light, in a place he didn't know a way out of.

As he watched, a face appeared in the window of the plane. He watched as it ran its hands down the window's glass. The spirit was terrified, and feared the coming of death, it had already experienced.

"You alright? What are you staring at?" Amelia asked him.

Daniel replied. "Nothing I can do anything about. It is too late to help them now."

"You are an angel. Can you see more of what is going on over there?" She asked.

"Yeah, I can see more than I ever wanted to, and there is not a damn thing I can do about it." Daniel said sinking lower into his seat.

The plane of the dead flew forward and continued its fall from the sky. Although its engines were still functioning, there was no one to pull the plane up out of a crash. Amelia became upset wishing she could stop the plane from crashing and possibly hurting those on the ground.

"Amelia, if I were over there, could you talk me through landing that plane?"

"Are you nuts. You can't get on that plane. Or can you?"

"I can get there, but I don't know how to land a plane."

"Maybe you don't have to, if you could pull it up and slow it down. Could you get out as it hit the ground?"

"Yes, I can orb away from the plane at the last second." Daniel became nervous, he knew there was little time."

"Then do it, and get their radio on. I will help you along the way."

Daniel looked at the other planes cockpit and drew on his nervous energy. As a blue light surrounded him, he disappeared from the seat of the Lockheed Electra and appeared in the other plane. Quickly he moved a pilot out of his seat, and grabbed a headset and began to call to Amelia.

"Daniel, grab the yoke, and pull back, to bring the nose of the plane up. We need to level you off." Amelia used her knowledge to coax Daniel through her attempt to land. Although the instruments were advanced, the principles were still the same, and Daniel brought the plane under control and aimed it away from signs of life. His final act before orbing out, was to level the plane, and extend its landing gear, just as it touched ground.

Daniel reappeared alongside Amelia as the plane bounced along the sand covered ground. They watched in amazement of how little damage there was. The plane was intact as it stopped rolling.

"You did good kid." Amelia said as she tried to comfort him.

"I did nothing, but save a few more lives. There was nothing I could have done for them. I just wonder how they died. Better yet, how did they get here through a portal? This seems so engineered. Like the work of a sandman. I want to go on that plane. I need answers." Daniel was not willing to give up so easily.

Chapter Ten

Tale of the Body Snatchers

As soon as Amelia opened the door of her plane. Daniel hit the ground, on his way towards the crashed hulk before him. Zach made his way to them, trying to catch Daniel, still unaware of what they had just encountered. He called out Daniel's name, trying to stop him if only for a moment.

"What the hell is going on?" Zach yelled as he grabbed for Daniel's arm.

"The plane just came through a portal." Daniel answered.

"So, there have been all kinds of planes landing here." Zach replied.

"Yeah, but this one is filled with dead people."

"What do you mean dead? If they are dead, then who landed that thing?"

"Daniel did." Amelia said as she came up from behind.

"You can fly a plane?" Zach said to him in a state of confusion.

"No, I cannot fly a plane. Amelia can fly a plane and she talked me through it enough to crash land. Look, there is no way a flight full of dead people made it through a portal. Someone helped this, and if I put money on it, I would bet it was the sandmen,"

"Well, I guess we will never know, being they are all dead." Zach said trying to end the situation.

"Wrong. I was dead, and still have my abilities to talk to and see spirits. Someone on that flight still has the ability to communicate. I know I saw more than one ghost moving about." Daniel finished explaining and moved closer to the plane.

"Wait, there are spirits on that plane?" Amelia asked.

"Yes, and we are about to find out how they got to be spirits."

Daniel came up to the door of the plane and looked at it. He turned back to the others and shook his head. "I think this is something I best do alone." Then he turned back to the plane, and a flash of blue light engulfed his body.

Inside the plane, he reappeared deep in the rows of passenger seats. He turned and looked all around, at the bodies thrown about as the plane landed. Many were still in their seats with their seatbelts fastened.

As he studied the bodies, he expected to see some movement, any would have been welcomed. Walking towards the front of the plane, he stared back and forth. He knew there were ghosts, he just didn't know why they were scared of him.

As Daniel arrived at the door to the cockpit, he reached for the handle just as it was pulled out of his hand. As the door flew open, Daniel came face to face with one of the pilots. He remembered the man's face, since it was the body Daniel had to remove from his chair to fly the plane.

"Who are you?" The man asked.

"I am Daniel, I came here to help."

"Sorry my friend, you cannot help the dead." The man replied.

"Maybe, maybe not. Look, I need to know what happened here. How did all these people die?" Daniel asked.

"I don't know. When we took off, everyone was fine. Then half way through our flight, I got up to stretch my legs. When I looked back here, they were all dead. They looked as if they were frozen in their seats. Even the attendants were dead. There is no way to explain this." He finished.

"Then what happened to you?"

"When I got back and told the copilot what was going on, it was like a bright light hit us. It felt like I was being shaken apart from the inside. Then I felt the plane surge downwards and we passed through the weird opening where the outside world changed. It was the last thing I saw before I died."

"There is no way all these people died at the same time, and you lived past it." Daniel became frustrated.

"It didn't happen that way. He wasn't here when the other men were." Daniel turned to see a small girl behind him. He kneeled down on one knee and looked her in the face. The child was scared and confused; she did not understand why she was dead.

"What men were here sweetheart?" Daniel asked.

"The men with the funny glasses and the sand bags. They brought us here. We were in a different place before this. Something bad happened to us before they came."

"Do you know what happened or where you were before?"

"We were in a big building, and there was a weird smell. People started to get sick and cough. Then they started to fall. My mom was there with me. I think she is dead. Then these men came and took all the people and made a pile, before they took them away."

"So, how did you get here?" Daniel spoke softly, trying to be patient.

"The weird men brought us here, and put us in these seats as the people from the plane were taken away. They didn't look sick or dead."

Daniel turned to the pilot with a look of fear. "Could someone have switched these people out while you were flying?"

"I did notice some weird jerking of the plane, like something heavy was shifting. I just thought it was turbulence."

"No, it was a whole group of people getting kidnapped by the sandmen. That is a hell of a way to recruit warm bodies. They probably never thought the plane would land here. If the plane crashed with the right number of bodies, who would question if they burned up? Instead, your plane fell through a portal to another universe."

"You mean we are not on earth anymore?" he asked.

"Look outside the window and see for yourself. This is a whole other place. And for now, we are stuck here …living and dead." Daniel said as he looked through the window to the people waiting below for answers.

Mullins

Chapter Eleven

Secrets of the Map

Daniel departed the plane and appeared on the ground. In front of him, were a group of confused people who did not need more bad news, and sadly he had to be the bearer. He walked over with a solum look on his face.

"I don't like that look." Amelia said under her breath.

"Me either, but as I have come to know him, there is a reason." Zach replied.

"There were spirits on board, but that is not the big news."

"What do you mean?" Amelia interrupted him.

"When the plane took off, there were living people onboard. In the course of the flight, there were all exchanged for the dead onboard. Only the pilots died during the flight. They were never meant to be here; they just fell through a portal accidentally. They were meant to crash and the end result would be a bunch of burned bodies that were unrecognizable."

"Why would someone do that?" Zach did not understand.

"Being the people were changed out in midflight, I would say the sandmen were recruiting new members. I mean, think about it. If the people were removed and everyone thought they were dead, what better way to grow your ranks. There were no living witnesses. The people's relatives would just thing they were killed in the crash. No damage to the timeline or dealing with missing persons." Daniel paced as he told his idea.

"We have to get out of here and stop them." Zach tried to contain his anger, as he spoke.

"Easier said than done. We don't have any way of finding the portals." Amelia added.

"Ah, but that is where you are wrong. While you were flying about surveying everything, I made a discovery. A pretty big one, I think."

Zach led them to an area where the light was bright, and pulled his sand bag around. Reaching to the side of it, he pulled forth a knife that was hidden in a side holder. He held it up and showed Daniel.

"So, how does that help us?" Daniel spoke up.

"Watch my friend, and learn."

As Zach held the end of the knife at an angle in the light, the area around him began to change. Projected to the air around, was a colorful map of the portal system, in the land of lost things. As he angled the knife, more regions began to show. Amelia looked on in aw, she had never seen anything like this before. She smiled and raised her hands to her mouth.

"This is our ticket home." Zach said being proud of his discovery.

"This is amazing Zach, but it shows the ways in, but are they also ways out?" Daniel asked.

"You mean doors don't always go both ways?" Amelia asked.

"It is possible, I really hope I am wrong though. The thing is, getting near enough to one of these to test it."

Maybe I could just fly us right up to one. With that nifty ability to transport yourself, you could get out."

"Yeah, but you would still be here." Daniel replied. "And we still have to deal with the entity possessing Jen. She has been too quiet."

"Don't worry, she'll be back." Zach said shaking his head.

"Do you always get what you wish for?" Amelia asked.

"What do you mean?" Zach questioned her.

"There is something in the distance coming up fast."

The big black energy bird, flew towards them, flapping its huge wings, and making a loud screeching sound, you could hear from over a mile away. Daniel turned to look at it, as he heard the voice inside his head. It was Jen, or something sounded like her. He felt his knees buckle as the sound of her voice filled his head.

Daniel felt a pain run through his body as he almost doubled over. Somehow, she was trying to pull energy from his body. Throwing up a shield, he tried to block her connection. Turning to look at Zach, he said. "You need to get the others to safety. She is coming back, and she is hungry."

Mullins

Chapter Twelve

Reunited

Daniel rose to his feet. He felt the energy being ripped from his body, but he was not going to just stand by and allow it to happen. Turning towards the black energy bird, he focused on his rapport and called out to the entity. His simple message, 'Not today."

As his message was delivered, so was a blast of energy that severed their connection. Daniel felt a shiver run down his spine, as his energy leveled out. He had been drained but not so much he could not defend himself.

He stared upwards as he extended his wings and rose into the air. As the enormous black bird flapped its wings, rain began to fall around them.

Daniel found it unexpected, since the place they were, was a desert terrain. Still the cool rain drops on his skin were a welcome relief from the heat.

Reaching a height where he was face to face with the entity, he floated and looked at the creature that was once the woman he loved. A confused pain filled his head and heart. He knew what he had to do, he just wished he did not feel so wrong in the act. The bird flapped its wings, as it began to drift closer to him.

"That's close enough. I know what you are doing." Daniel called out.

"I am not here to harm you." The entity responded.

"You have a funny way of showing it. I didn't appreciate the energy drain."

"I meant no harm. I was weak, and you have an endless source. It would not have done any real damage."

"My energy is mine to use and if I decided to share it, it would be my choice, not yours." Daniel snapped back.

"I understand. I am learning. I have learned much from this creature you call Jen. I do not understand your ways. To be human is an experience for me. So many sensations and feelings flooding me at once."

"You mean so many of Jen's experiences that you are stealing." Daniel wasn't going to let this go over easily.

"I did not mean to steal anything. When Jen orbed you all to safety, after the Queen captured you, I was near and watched. I saw the sandman pouring sand over you. Jen broke free to save you all, but her rush of energy would have killed her. As she entered the wormhole dragging you both, I followed. I wanted to help her." The deep dark voice of the bird echoed into Daniel's ears.

"Wait, you followed?" Daniel questioned. "Then it was you, who caused us to get stuck in this god-awful place. Jen only anticipated the three of us, you threw it all off. This is all your fault."

"No, you do not understand. Jen was losing consciousness when she orbed. You all would have died. If I did not merge with her, the wormhole would have failed and thrown you all to your deaths."

"Then why did you attack me and do all this?" Daniel wanted answers.

"I was confused at first and the power was welcome. I liked what it did to me to share Jen's existence. I was lost in the sensations, and I did not want to let go. I still do not. I do understand it is wrong. I just don't want to let go of this life I am creating."

The entity threw its wings back, and reached out its claws grabbing ahold of Daniel. As it flapped its wings harder, it climbed higher into the sky. The rain pelted them hard, as a scream emerged from the bird. Daniel tried to free himself by creating a shield around him, but the bird's claws just grabbed harder, forcing air from his lungs.

As they reached a high point, the bird stopped and Daniel studied his situation. Looking upwards, he noticed something he could not see from the ground. Just behind the clouds, was a glowing line. Daniel cocked his head and thought, 'a portal." He studied it, not trying to let on to what he was seeing.

"Why are you so quiet all of a sudden?" The entity asked.

"Do I have a choice to speak? You seem to want to control everything."

"No, that is not what I want. I do not know, what I want. I am confused, it is hard to sort my own thoughts out from Jen's. So many of her feelings are carrying over to me. I have never experienced these emotions, these feelings of love."

Daniel looked to the entity. He finally knew what was happening. The entity was in love with him. She did not know how to deal with the intensity, of what humans live through all their lives. This creature had just revealed its weakness to him. Daniel had just been handed the upper hand.

"Let me go." Daniel demanded.

"Then you will leave me."

"No, I am not going anywhere." Daniel replied.

The entity was confused, she did not know what to do. Deep inside, Jen called out to her convincing her to release her grip. Daniel smiled as he heard Jen's message. She was still in there, still alive.

As the claws released, Daniel floated backwards. He studied the bird for a moment. He had to be careful, or he would lose his advantage. He subtly looked off into the distance. The light from the opening was still there. As he looked on, he could see the entire opening looking like a huge rectangle in the sky. Perhaps, he thought, this is our way out.

"I have angered you, haven't I?" The entity asked.

"No, I was just catching my breath. I have been up here too long, I need rest." He lied.

The entity was more confused than ever, she was having trouble distinguishing herself from Jen's memories. The two had been intertwined too long. It was if the entity was starting to believe she was Jen. Being human, was too much for a being who had no idea how to absorb it all.

Daniel looked into the entity's eyes, as he spoke. "I understand what you are feeling. It is so much to take on. You need a moment to process and rest. So do I, then we can meet again and plan where we go from here." Daniel faked a smile. "Are you OK with that?"

"Yes, we need time. I will come back tomorrow and we will be together again."

The bird backed off and floated away, watching Daniel as it prepared to leave. He continued to smile, as the bird disappeared into the distance. Daniel felt the outrage surge through him as he turned away. This creature had stolen Jen's life, feelings and emotions. He could only imagine Jen's feelings of violation.

As he turned, he headed for the energy outline in the sky. The closer he came to it, the more his powers began to falter. Something about the portal was draining him. Daniel realized the level of drain, as he began to fall from the sky. As Daniel plummeted downwards, his wings fluttered out of control. He knew this was going to hurt, as he flew towards the ground.

Chapter Thirteen

On the Wings of a Bird

As Daniel spun around, falling from the sky, he watched his wings fade, disappearing from sight. He watched as the sand came closer, with his power gone, he was helpless.

From the ground, Zach looked up to him. He realized Daniel had no control. He had to do something to save his friend. It could not end like this. Reaching for his sand bag, he rummaged through, looking for something that could help. Since he received the bag, he had learned so much about using it and the power within, but this was a situation he had never faced.

The bag filled with sand, had so much power, but sand could not stop a person falling from the sky. The small knife was another matter, it had power,

Zach felt it as he held the knife and saw its ability to show the portals.

He pulled the knife out by its handle, that showed the mark of the sandmen. Holding the knife by the end and raising it into the sky, he felt a tingling in his hand. It started out low and then grew. There was a power being emitted from the knife.

He knew with all the abilities the sandmen had, there was an element of focus that had to be applied whenever directing a power. When he used the sand, he envisioned the goal he had, so with the knife he tried the same thing. He looked to Daniel and focused on saving him.

The knife began to glow and got brighter the harder Zach wished. The glow became blinding, as it shot forward towards the sky. The rain flew harder towards the ground, as the light of the knife cut through the sky. As it reached Daniel, his fall slowed.

Daniel screamed as he fell, closing his eyes not knowing what this event would do to him. He was dead after-all, an angel. He should survive anything, but there were no guarantees. As the beam hit him, Daniel's fall slowed. He slowly opened his eyes and looked down at the light that had formed a platform under his body.

Daniel could see Zach with his hand extended controlling the knife. He screamed out and laughed, as he believed he might survive this. Zach guided the beam down, towards the sand near Amelia's plane.

As Daniel neared the ground, Amelia followed by Fred, walked towards him. "You alright Kid?" Amelia yelled out to him.

"Yeah, I think so. As good as can be expected." Daniel responded.

"What the hell happened to you?" Fred spoke with a sigh of relief.

"Did the entity drain you?" Amelia asked.

"No, I was OK after she left. Then I flew higher towards the light in the sky that looked like a portal opening. Then I lost all of my power. I don't know how to explain it." Daniel replied.

Zach ran over to them still holding the knife in his hand. Daniel turned to him and smiled. He looked down to the knife. Reaching out he took it in his hand and studied it. Such a small thing saved his life. He did not understand how to comprehend the power of the sandmen.

"So, this is what saved me. How did you know?" Daniel asked.

"I didn't, I just had to do something. I searched the sandbag and this was the only thing I knew had power to do odd things."

"You said it could show a map of all the portals?" Daniel questioned.

"Yeah, it can display a map for wherever you are. Watch this." Zach said as he raised the knife upwards.

From within the knife a light began to emit. In front of the group, a lighted screen appeared in the air. The landscape appeared after, above there were shapes indicating where each opening was. Daniel looked hard as the shape appeared in the clouds above their location.

"I knew it. Directly above us, is a portal. I was sure it was, there is an outline of the opening sides."

"That is amazing news. Then we have a way to get out of here." Zach became excited.

"Don't get too excited just yet. I got close to that thing and it drained all my power. That is why I was falling like a rock out of the sky." Daniel said as he looked upwards.

"Besides, we don't know where that goes. All of us here are from different times and places. What if that opening goes to the past, or another place we end up trapped. It's a big risk to go through. We need more information." Amelia tried to be the voice of reason.

"I understand what you are saying and I agree. I also understand we cannot stay here forever just hoping and wondering. We need to get out of here. The sandmen could already be starting their attack on earth." Zach tried to make his point clear.

"We don't even know if we can go through the opening. It may be a one-way door. It might not open." Daniel added.

"Then we test it." Amelia added. "If we have to do this, then we prepare and gather information." Amelia said, realizing they had been there long enough. She had been in this place for over 80 years. It was time to go home, no matter what time period it was in.

Chapter Fourteen

Mission Impossible

Amelia looked to the sky. That place had been her home for so many years. Even as a child she dreamed of flight. She remembered her childhood, back then they called her "Meeley." She spent so many hours with her younger sister named Grace, who was nicknamed "Pidge." Amelia put together a home-made ramp, constructed like a roller coaster she had seen on a trip to St. Louis.

Amelia's well-documented first flight ended in a crash. She emerged from the broken wooden box that had served as a transport, with a bruised lip, ripped dress and a "sensation of exhilaration". She exclaimed, "Oh, Pidge, it's just like flying!" From that point she feared nothing and could not be held back.

"Oh Pidge, I had almost forgotten you in all this time I have spent here." Amelia spoke under her breath.

"Who is Pidge?" Daniel asked.

"Oh, sorry about that, I was talking out loud and remembering my life on earth." Amelia's voice quivered as she wiped a tear from her eye. "I was just thinking of my sister Grace, her nickname was Pidge, and we were inseparable as children. Since I came here, I seem to have forgotten so many of the people in my life. I guess if we went back in the present day, they would all be dead and gone. I know we can't go home again. But if it has to be present day, that is better than here."

"I happen to know a little bit about being out of place. I am more than seventy years out of time. It isn't easy, but you can adjust. I did, and I have so many people I have adopted as family. You just have to keep the ones you loved in your heart, and make room for new people in there as well." Daniel smiled as he reached out to take hold of Zach's shoulder.

"How long have you two known each other?" Amelia asked.

"Not all that long, but Zach has joined my little family. Sometimes, you just hold on to those who you bond with." Daniel smiled at Amelia. "You already have someone in this new life."

Amelia understood Daniel's sentiment. His words were not waisted as she smiled back at him, in her huge tomboy way. She reached out and took his hand and held on. "You are quite an amazing kid, you know?"

Daniel held tight to Amelia as he walked her over and looked up to where the portal opening was. He needed to get back to it and find out if it was only one way. He studied the sky, as he wondered how to get there, and if he did, what about Jen? He had to free her. He was torn on his feelings of handling that problem.

As Zach walked to them, he pulled the knife out and aimed it upwards. As he did, a light emitted from the knife. It was different from before, and

Zach did not call on it to happen. The light went forth to the opening in the sky. It was if the knife was receiving information.

The doorway changed, and they could see the opening. The door was allowing something to pass through. From above, a single engine craft flew past. As it fell from the sky, it ripped through the air just above them. Daniel tried to transport himself near the plane, but he was still too weak.

"My special boy, you cannot win them all. That one, is simply one of those things you could not control. For now, you need rest and food. That isn't the first plane to rip through the gate and land here and it will probably not be the last. Now come back to the plane and I will make you up a bed. You can sack out, and I will get some food in you."

Daniel did not complain as Amelia led him to the plane. She walked past Zach and looked over her shoulder. "Well, are you coming?" She laughed. Zach ran behind and caught up with them. Amelia had achieved something she never thought she would in life, she had a couple of kids to care for. She had thought about it in her past life, but it never really suited her. Her life was too busy and filled with adventures. With the current situation, this just seemed right.

As Daniel settled in to rest, Amelia watched over him like a mother. From the moment he closed his eyes, he started to dream. It his dream he relived his past at the moment just before he died. His time with Amelia must have triggered it all. He dreamed of the woman who was supposed to have been his mother. It was at her hands he died.

~~~~

"Mom, why are you being so crazy about this? I just want to know the truth." Daniel pleaded with Emily, but she became outraged. The final threads of the lie she and her husband had hidden for sixteen years was unraveling. Daniel had stumbled onto the truth. Being a head strong teenager meant he was not going to give up easy and let it rest.
~~~~

"Daniel, sometimes the past is better left in the past. Why won't you just leave this all alone before you cause more problems than ever imagined." Emily pleaded with him.

"No, I want the truth. Is the woman I saw with dad, my mother, or are you. I am tired of being lied to. I have felt my whole life something was wrong. I don't know how but I have always known, didn't you see how as a child I would never call you Mommy? Damn-it tell me the truth."

"Ok, you want the truth, then I will give it to you. You are not my son. You are the bastard child of my husband and his secretary. While I was home being the loving and devoted wife, your dad was out screwing the help. He thought he wouldn't get caught. Well guess what, when you get another woman pregnant, then…you get caught. At least my children will be born into a house of marriage." Emily spewed forth all the hatred she had pushed down for so long.

Emily reveled in delight as she unloaded years of pain and hatred. She never thought about the fact it was aimed at an innocent boy. Emily's husband should have been her target instead of an innocent sixteen-year-old, who bore the load of his father's sin.

Daniel stared on in disbelief as he tried to conceive how such a thing could be true. The man he had loved and respected his whole life had been living a lie. What was worse, he had made Daniel live that lie as well. His whole world began to crash around him. Nothing and no one he ever believed in was real anymore. They were just a group of actors, each one playing the roles they assigned themselves.

A tear ran down Daniel's face, as he looked into Emily's eyes. She was as much a victim as he was. Confusion filled his mind, as he searched for any clear way to accept any of it. All he knew was that he wanted to get out of the house of lies that was closing in around him. He turned and headed for the door, as a look of terror crept across Emily's face. Her only thought was. 'What have I done?'

Daniel raced for the door before Emily could plead with him not to go. She knew what she had done was wrong. She knew when James came home from work, there would be hell to pay for this. She had to fix it. She had to keep Daniel at home, and persuade him not to tell his father what he found out.

Emily raced for the door and grabbed her keys. Daniel had to be nearby, there wasn't enough time for him to get far. As Emily raised the garage door, the rain poured on her head. She worked quickly to get down the drive. In her confusion, she backed the car into the side porch, before squealing tires and heading for the main road.

As she drove, the rain pelted her windshield. The old wipers were too shredded to keep the window clear. Emily could barely see as the tears burned her eyes, and the windshield started to fog over. Rounding the corner, she didn't see Daniel walking by the road. As she tried to wipe the windshield, the car swerved towards the edge of the road.

As Daniel heard the sound of the car coming at him, it was too late to move. He looked into the headlight's bright white glow, as the car ran him down. As he fell to the ground unconscious, his last thoughts were almost humorous. He started life as an accident and now he would die that same way.

Emily jumped from the car and ran to his side. Time stopped for her in that moment. Everything around her froze, as she felt the pain hit her heart so hard it was going to explode. She screamed out for help, hoping someone, anyone would hear her. Emily just sat there in her frozen state cradling Daniel in her arms. She only whispered in Daniel's ear, "I am so sorry…I was wrong."

As a siren in the distance filled the air, Emily knew she had to go. Fear gripped her as she gently moved Daniel's head onto the roadside. She could hear voices in the distance, the neighbors must have called the police. She knew if she was caught, her life would be over.

Turning towards the car, Emily clawed her way back to her feet. Without thinking, she started the car and screeched off down the wet road. As the rain pounded on the windshield, her tears ran down her face dragging lines of mascara with them. Looking in the rear-view mirror, she saw the lights of the police car, not coming for her, but stopping along the roadside, where Daniel's body had been left. Breathing a sigh of relief, she knew they had found him, and for the moment she was safe.

~~~~

As Daniel's dream reached its conclusion, he sat up with a scream. He would never be able to accept what happened. Since his death, and his understanding of the afterlife, he was even more angry, that he had no closure. He would never see Emily again, or tell her what he really thought. And with that, he became angry.
~~~~

She was the reason he did not trust, and why he struggled to love Jen. It was because of her, he wanted to be a part of Amelia's life. To see how a healthy relationship could be, with a woman who just wanted to be a mother, with no strings attached. With Daniel's anger, he felt a surge in his power. His strength had returned, and so had his determination to get out of the Land of Lost Things.

Mullins

Chapter Fifteen

Identity Thief

The entity rested from its last encounter with Daniel. It had regained its strength and retained its hold over Jen. Deep within, Jen sat back watching and studying the creature's movements. She knew it had a weak point somewhere. So far, its weakest link was Daniel.

Since the entity imprinted all of Jen's traits onto itself, it also adopted the love she shared with him. 'That's it!' Jen thought to herself. The one thing it wants is Daniel.

Jen pulled on every bit of energy she could muster while the creature slept. She had to contact Daniel. As she tapped into the rapport they shared, the creature stirred, but did not wake up. Daniel sat up as he felt the message coming from Jen.

"Daniel, can you hear me?" Jen called out.

"Yes Jen, how is this possible?" He asked.

"She is sleeping. I don't know how long I have. Look, you have the advantage, she copied all my memories and my feelings for you, Use it against her. If you weaken her, maybe Zach can pull something out of the sandman bag, to separate her from me."

"Maybe there is a way. I need to talk to Zach about it."

"Do whatever you have to. I am tired of being a passenger in my own body. Oh, do me a favor." Jen stopped for a second.

"Sure, anything, what do you want me to do."

"When you take her down. Make it hurt." Jen's voice was filled with anger.

"I understand." Daniel said knowing exactly what she meant.

As Jen finished sending her message, the creature began to awaken. Jen had finished just in time. As the entity sat up, she realized Jen had been active for some time. As she gathered her focus, she thought of Daniel.

"Were you calling out to him as I slept?" The entity became enraged.

"You'll never know." Jen teased her, she knew what she was doing, she wanted the creature enraged. "Payback is a bitch, isn't it?"

Daniel got Zach's attention, who had just been lying there with his eyes shut, trying to figure the situation out. As Daniel sat down beside him, Zach propped himself up on his arm. They both knew it was time to take charge of the situation

"Jen just contacted me."

"I figured as much. Your dream was pretty violent and when it stopped you got quieter as if you were in a different place." Zach responded.

"Jen says we have the upper hand with the creature. It has all her feelings and memories. So, if we hit it hard with her feelings for me, we will win."

"Yes, but how do we convince it to leave her body?" Zach said as he laid back on his pillow.

That's where you come in. That knife has all this power going on. Can you wield it to rip the entity from Jen's body?" Daniel asked.

"I don't know how to do that. What if I hurt Jen?" Zach sat up in a panic.

"If you hurt her physically, I can heal her. I have that ability. Let's just hope it does not come to that." Daniel tried to reassure him.

"Daniel, there has to be another way."

"Trust me, there isn't. We have to do this, or we cannot leave this place. I won't go without Jen. And until this is settled, we are stuck here."

"Ok, I will do it, but I won't like it." Zach moaned. "So, when do we start?"

"Now, no time like the present." Daniel said as he gathered himself and prepared to go outside.

Daniel left the plane, with Zach close behind him. He studied the area, checking to see if everything was OK after his time sleeping. For the first time since they arrived there, he was sure about what he was doing.

"Did you get some rest?" Amelia asked.

"Yes, I think, but that is not important right now. It is time to go bird hunting. I think we have a way of setting Jen free."

"That's all good, but what do you do with the entity when you tear it out of her body?" Amelia asked.

"You have a good point. I am not one to take a life. We can't let it possess another person." Daniel thought for a second. "Where do we send it?"

"I'd say send it through the portal. We don't know what that will do to a person. Be nice to have a guinea pig ready for the test." Amelia made a face with a crooked smile. "Let's get to it."

"Could you fly your plane with a person on the wing?" Daniel asked.

"Wait, are you crazy?" Zach felt a chill run through him.

"I agree with him, are you crazy?"

"No, it is easier to confront her in the air. Besides, I want to get a closer look at the portal. On top of the plane, I can do it without falling to my death.

Daniel turned and walked towards the plane. The others ran behind him, they knew there was no use in fighting with him. His mind was made up. Boarding the plane, they all knew this was dangerous even for an angel.

Amelia began her check of all the systems before taking off. She fired up the engines, as she checked the area for anything in the way of her liftoff. She turned to look at Daniel, as he took his place to her side in the co-pilot's seat. She would do anything to protect him, but he was asking too much of them this time.

As the plan rolled across the sand, they began to gain speed and shortly after, the wheels left the ground. Amelia said a silent prayer in her head to protect them, especially Daniel.

As the plane climbed to the altitude needed, Daniel scanned for the opening. The plane flew towards it, as he caught sight of the lighted rim. It was just ahead. Daniel told Amelia to lower the plane to just under the opening.

As she steadied the plane, Daniel climbed out of his seat. He spoke. "Wish me luck." With a quick movement, he disappeared from the cockpit and reappeared kneeling on the top of the right wing.

Reaching a hand upwards, he touched the opening of the portal. At first, he felt nothing, then the sting of energy charged through his fingertips. He was not sure what this meant, but he was sure they were right. The opening to get out was just above them.

As Daniel was about to orb back to his seat inside the plane, he heard the all too familiar sound of the black energy bird. The entity was coming up quickly behind him. Daniel looked on in fear, of what she could do to the plane, and the others inside. He had to get them to safety before he could initiate their plan to take her down.

Amelia saw the dark energy coming from behind as she turned the plane and headed back to the ground. Just below the portal, Daniel rose up off the metal surface and extended his wings. It was time to reclaim Jen.

Chapter Sixteen

Like a Goddess

As Daniel floated in the sky with the winds whipping around him, he thought back to his first days of having power. He was so unprepared for his abilities. When he realized what he could do with just the thought of his mind, he was terrified.

He was destined to be a White-Lighter, but his course was altered in life. When he ended up in the cemetery, he started down a different path. He should have been trained by higher level guardians. Instead, he chose a path to protect Jen, and save her from a life that was unraveling before her. He never regretted that choice.

As he watched the bird grow nearer, he realized this would not end well. If the entity resisted him, he would end up having to use the power he developed, on the one person he loved. He wasn't prepared for that; no more than he was prepared for the first battle he had with the Dark-Lighter. The memory flew through his mind. He felt his heart pound as the image of the one called Malachi forced its way into his thoughts.

~~~~~

The Guardian Angel Elizabeth watched as the Dark-Lighter spread his black mist across the cemetery. She wanted to intervene, but to do so would go against the rules of good and evil. She could not break the balance of power. If anyone was to fight this fight, it would have to be Daniel. Elizabeth lowered her eyes, as she had watched this scenario over and over again in her head, to see all the possible outcomes. No matter how it played out, someone would die during this battle. To maintain the balance, a death was necessary.
~~~~~

"You are watching him again." The man's voice came from behind.

"Yes, the dark-lighter has returned. Daniel is not ready." Elizabeth said in a distressed voice.

"Then help him be ready." The Guardian urged her.

"I am not allowed to interfere that way. I can only help him, if he does not know I am doing it. He will one day be a god, but for now he has to remain a spirit. If his spirit is to die, I can intervene, but I cannot fight his battles for him."

"So, the High One has spoken about this?"

"Yes, I can intervene to save his life, but the rules still apply."

"Perhaps, just pay attention, and if Daniel needs a nudge, give him a subtle one. I would, if he was my charge."

"Point taken. I will watch and do what I have to."

<p style="text-align:center">~~~</p>

Daniel walked out of the door of the chapel. His face hid the fear he had buried deep inside himself. If this was his day to die again as a spirit, then he would face it head on. As he neared, the Dark-Lighter turned to him. A sinister smile crossed his face. It was a look of condescension.

"Oh, it's you again. Come back to spread your light over the cemetery."

"Come back? I never left." Daniel jabbed at him.

"What do you hope to gain by coming back here? The spirits will not leave with you. They have agreed to wait for the light."

"Maybe…but with a little persuasion, you can change anyone's mind."

"Not going to happen. I think it is your time to leave and not come back."

The Dark-Lighter turned from Daniel, and resumed the mist, that now covered most of the lower cemetery. He paid no attention to Daniel's movements. It was a mistake on the Dark-Lighter's part, and the more Daniel was ignored, the angrier he became. Deep inside, Daniel felt the power building. He had only known the feeling of an orb happening, but this was different. This was stronger.

Abigail came up from behind Daniel and touched his shoulder. "Do what you have to do. He is wrong, and if you can make it right…you should." Daniel looked at her and knew what she meant. This had to end.

"I told you to leave, and if I have to, I will help you to go." Daniel sounded more determined than ever.

The Dark-Lighter turned to face him. He was done playing games with the White-Lighter. He was ready for the fight. He breathed deeply and cocked his head. "You know what Dark-Lighters do best? We kill want-to-be angels like you." He pulled his arms apart, as his energy formed a dark bow in his hands. The arrow formed as he aimed towards Daniel. "Ready to die White-Lighter?"

Abigail watched as the Dark-Lighter took aim. As Daniel tried to focus his energy, Abigail could tell something was wrong. The arrow flew from the bow towards its mark. As his eyes grew wide, a look of fear crossed Daniel's face and he prepared for the worse. Above, Elizabeth looked on in terror, as she prepared to intervene.

Time slowed to a crawl as the arrow flew from its source. As it came inches from hitting its mark, Abigail took a deep breath and knew she had to intervene. She threw herself in front of Daniel, in the final seconds. He looked at her in disbelief as she fell to the ground. The arrow killed as it was intended, but the wrong innocent spirit was claimed. It pierced through her chest, creating a dark void where it passed.

"No!" Daniel cried out, as she fell into his arms. "Why did you do this?"

"You got better things waiting for you. I just have the light. I can see it now, you know." Abigail smiled at Daniel as she spoke. "You were right.

Mama is there waiting for me. She is calling me to come home with her."

"Abigail, I don't know how to thank you."

"You don't have to, I got what I waited for so long. Now you gotta fight him hard. And one day, I will see you again. You'll always be my friend."

With Abigail's last words, she faded away and Daniel's rage intensified. As Daniel stood up, a tear ran down his cheek. He was done playing with the Dark-Lighter. If it was a war he wanted, then it was a war he would get.

"I don't know what makes you think you have the right to kill an innocent."

"It is in my nature. It's just what I do. I meant to kill you, but your friend got in the way. Now I will correct that mistake, and finish what I started."

Daniel clinched his fist in rage, the power inside him filled his whole system. As Malachi pulled his bow again, Daniel began to glow. The arrow formed and was releasing, just as Daniel pulled back his arms, and released an enormous blast of energy. As he aimed at the Dark-Lighter, the arrow disintegrated and the force of the blast knocked Malachi to his knees.

"So, you aren't quite as defenseless as I was led to believe."

The Dark-Lighter stumbled to his feet, and summoned all the power he had within him. The force flew from him like a black wall heading for Daniel. As it hit, he flew backwards slamming his head against a tombstone. Daniel stumbled back to his feet, regaining his focus just as a second wave of dark energy came at him. This time he was ready, releasing a wave of his own energy. The two blasts met between them and held in equal force. As they pushed towards each other, their blasts shot energy out all around them and obliterated everything it touched.

The Dark-Lighter tried to increase his energy, as he felt Daniel getting stronger. Malachi was losing the battle, and he was sure it would not be long before he was finished. Daniel walked towards him, getting stronger with every step. He could not imagine having this level of energy within him, and his rage was growing out of control.

With a huge final blow, he threw everything he could muster at the Dark-Lighter. Malachi fell to the ground, his body was charred black, his clothing smoked and burned around him. Daniel had won. Malachi used the last of his energy, to phase out to a hiding place.

It was over, but Daniel's anger did not subside. It was all clear to him now, he was dead. His family and friends would move on without him. His newest friend Abigail, fell because of him. There was nothing left for him, but to wonder a cemetery waiting for the light, which may or may not come for him.

He fell to his knees and screamed as he felt the power building once again within him. He was out of control. Elizabeth watched him, as she orbed to the cemetery. She materialized just feet away, as

Daniel's power blast spread in all directions. All of his force hit the cemetery as the land around him went up in flames.

Elizabeth watched in fear of what he was doing, and for what he would become if he went unchecked. "Daniel, forgive me for what I am about to do. I will make this up to you one day, I promise you." Elizabeth lowered her shield, and as tears formed in her eyes, and she blasted Daniel with a pure white light only an angel could emit.

Daniel fell to the ground and lay unconscious. His body was burned and battered, but his power was contained. Elizabeth walked over and kneeled at his side. "I had to do this. If not, you would have destroyed this whole area. I will fix it though, and make things right. But I think it is best you don't remember much of this. You need to learn to master your power and abilities. It's not safe for you to learn on your own. For now, I am going to have to wipe these memories from you. You will just have a bit of your past, and a cloudy memory of your death and waking up here. In the years to come, it will return to you when the time is right. Just not now."

Elizabeth ran her hand over Daniel's head as a white light emerged coating his skin. After hiding his memories, she coated his entire body in a light to heal him. Daniel lay on the ground unaware he had been healed or changed.

Elizabeth headed away, out of the line of his site, in case he woke up, and for a while she watched him. She wondered what he would be like, when he attained full power as a god. For the moment he was safe, and back on track, and for that she was thankful.

Mullins

Chapter Seventeen

A Light in the Darkness

Daniel thought about his memory and remembered Elizabeth. She had come to be his mentor and greatest support, in the change from life to death, and back to life again. He missed her, but he realized from the memory, that everything is not easy. He battled the darkness before and won. He lost Abigail, but defeated Malachi. He had come so far and learned to master his power. Now the entity would learn that.

As Daniel watched, the large black bird stopped just feet from him. This time, he was more prepared. He was drained of power before, from the bird feeding off of him, and the portal draining what he had left. A smile crossed his face as he knew he was ready.

"You came back." Daniel said as he studied the giant black energy bird in front of him.

"It is time we stop fighting this. I know you love me. We will be together now. It's meant to be." The entity spoke in a loving but demented way.

Daniel played his part well, as he reached out his hand to her. He tried to do all the things Jen would have wanted him to do. Since the creature copied her thoughts and memories, he was sure this was what she would expect.

The bird moved closer and took his hand. She looked at him lovingly, as if she had done this with him a million times before. Inside, Jen kept her cool, she knew what Daniel was doing. She had to be quiet so the entity did not realize what was happening.

"I think the bird should go away for now. It is just us here. No need for the bird to be on display."

"You are right. It has been too long since we were together." The entity said, as she allowed the bird's form to disappear. "What now?"

Daniel looked at her for a moment, before taking her in his arms. He was careful to shield his energy from being absorbed. He was not going to play victim to that game again.

As he pulled her into an embrace, he looked over her shoulder. He could see Amelia's plane landing in the sand below them. They would be ready for him to make his next move.

The entity let go slightly from her embrace, and pulled her head back to look into his eyes. Daniel didn't know what to do as the dark one moved towards his lips. He had no choice, but to kiss her back, as he held tight and began to maneuver her downwards.

As they descended, Daniel held tight. It was working. As he looked into the creature's face, he saw the features of Jen, coated in the darkness of something he struggled to understand. He reminded himself that this creature had all these emotions and sensations thrust upon it. It did not ask for them. Perhaps it was not evil at all, just overpowered by the opportunity for life. He almost felt sorry for it, but then he remembered that the entity was holding Jen hostage.

As they landed on the ground, the entity realized what had happened. She let go of Daniel and stepped back. She was confused at why he had brought her there.

"What is going on? You and I were to be together. Alone…" She spoke in a dark psychotic sounding voice.

"We are going to be together. I just wanted to be on solid ground for a minute." Daniel lied.

He reached out to take her hand and she allowed him. He faked a smile at her, as he pretended to have interest. In the distance, he watched as Zach made his way towards them.

Zach did just as Daniel instructed him. As he approached, Zach was in stealth mode. He made no noise and stayed behind the entity at all times. He played his part perfectly. He was ready.

As Daniel held tight to the entity's hand, he tried to keep her attention on him, so she could not look around or see what was coming. "I've wanted the chance for us to be alone for so long now. Seems there has been so much going on in our lives, and the time we were separated was unbearable."

"That is all going to change now." She replied.

"Yes, I agree." Daniel said, as he gave the signal for Zach to come in from behind.

As Zach approached, the entity sensed his presence, but it was too late, as he had his knife out and ready. He held it into the air, and as it drew light from above, the energy was gathered and focused into an intense light beam.

Zach aimed his energy at the entity just as Daniel called upon his own power and aimed as well. The entity called forth her energy bird and prepared to climb into the sky again as the two attacked.

The bird struggled as its mighty wings flapped back and forth throwing sand and debris into the wind. Inside the entity, Jen began her own attack. She had little power, but she did have the ability to confuse and irritate the creature. As she mounted her attack, the entity lost all focus and could not aim her power.

As the bird swung its wings, Zach carefully got closer and the full power of the knife wrapped around the entity's form. He could feel the immense power of the knife hitting its mark. The bird was losing structure as the light energy disintegrated it.

Inside the entity, Jen felt the power that was holding her in place was weakening. As Daniel blasted the creature to the ground, he saw it splitting into two distinct forms. The entity was leaving Jen. He was sure of it.

"It's working Zach. They are separating. Just a little more." Daniel screamed.

And then the two figures were ripped apart. Jen fell to the side, as the entity stood up, and in its energy form, tried to escape. Jen pulled herself together, as she watched the being that had inhabited her body.

Struggling to gain control of her body again, Jen stood up and shakily moved closer. She looked at the pitiful creature and motioned for the boys to stop. As Daniel tried to move closer, Jen threw an energy shield towards him.

"This bitch is mine!" Jen screamed out, as she gained control over her power once more. "What in the hell makes you think you have the right to steal someone's life or body?" Jen said angrily.

"Not steal, I merely borrowed. Then, I became wrapped up in the life you had created. I never knew this was possible. I only meant to help you, when you were about to die. I never meant to become you."

"You never became me! You imitated. Nothing more." Jen growled as she pooled her power from within and prepared to unleash it.

"I am sorry for what I did. I just could not stop. Please show pity." The entity begged.

"You mean, like you showed me as you took my life and my existence." Jen was finished negotiating. "If I let you leave, you could go out and do this to someone else."

"No, I give you my word. I will not."

"Your word?" Jen began to laugh uncontrollably. As if I could ever trust you after what you did. This ends here."

As Jen pulled her arms back, her energy began to form, just not as before. From within her body, a bright yellow orange glow began to come forth. As it grew, it surrounded her body, and extended outwards.

Daniel backed up towards Zach as they watched what was happening. The energy collected and took form. Before them, Jen rose into the air. Around her body, the energy took shape. As Jen climbed higher, the form of a bright energy bird emerged. Its wings flapped outwards as it filled the sky above them. Jen had transformed into something she had never known possible. She, like the mighty Phoenix had been resurrected once more.

Mullins

Chapter Eighteen

Enter the Phoenix

"What is happening?" Amelia screamed out, as she and a group of the others joined Daniel and Zach. Jen rose higher into the air, and the full size of her energy bird shone above them. Looking on, no one knew if what they were seeing was a good sign or a bad one.

"Jen, what are you doing? "Daniel called out. "You are free now; this is not necessary."

Jen looked down to him. Her eyes were filled with a fiery energy. She acted as if she did not recognize him. Reaching down with a birdlike claw, she lifted him up. As they came eye to eye, she looked at him as if she vaguely remembered who he was.

"Jen, please stop this. You are free now. You don't have to do this." Daniel pleaded with her.

Jen looked Daniel in the face. Her memory was returning. She knew him again. He was the man she loved. It was all coming back to her now. She let go of the tight grip she had, and let him gently hang in her grasp.

"Someone has to pay for what was done to me." She said in anger.

"Jen, you won. She is defeated. The power she took from you has been diminished. She is just a powerless entity now. You don't have to destroy her."

"You could be right. I am so much more powerful than I was before. I don't understand what is happening to me. Why am I like this now?" Jen demanded answers.

"I think the entity tore down barriers in your mind. You were limited before, and the mix of your body with the entity, turned lose more power in you than you were ready for. We will just have to work together to manage it now." Daniel spoke as he tried to take it all in.

Daniel looked deep into her eyes which had started to revert to normal. Jen was becoming less goddess and more herself. He reached out to her and took her hands, as the energy bird started to fade.

As they came closer, their arms moved into an embrace. Everything the entity tried to copy, but could not, was there again. Daniel felt the love of Jen. She was back, just not the same as before.

Jen held tight to Daniel, as her power disappeared. He held her in the air as they kissed. "Hi blue eyes." She whispered to him. "Hello yourself. I am so glad you are back." Daniel replied.

As they held tight, their bodies spun around in a circle, slowly drifting to the ground. Jen smiled, as she realized she was back in charge of her own life. She looked over Daniel's shoulder to see the crowd below, and the entity which looked back at her.

Zach ran to them as they touched the ground. Jen turned to him as he called out to her. They hugged hard, harder than they ever had before. He smiled at her as she reached out a hand to touch his face. She was happy they had all survived the trip there, as well as the entity.

As she scanned the crowd, Jen turned to the creature that hung back and away from the others. Jen walked towards her, as the creature cowered out of sight of the others. Jen was still angry, and she would get her chance to be face to face with the entity.

"Cowering in the corner out of the way. So different than when we shared the same body. You were so in control then. Not so strong, when you are not possessing my body, are you?" Jen snapped at her.

"I meant no harm. I swear." She responded.

"You meant harm. Don't lie. If my friends had not freed me, you would have stolen my whole life." Jen became enraged.

"No, please have mercy on me." The entity begged.

"You mean, like you did with me? Oh wait, you showed me no mercy. You wanted everything that was mine. I won't let this happen to anyone else." As Jen spoke her voice turned harsh and echoed.

As the entity crawled backwards, Jen came closer. As she breathed deeply, she summoned the power that was in her. It was different now, so much stronger. As she reached out her hand, and turned it palm upwards, a ball of energy formed within it.

As she bounced the ball up and down in her hand, she watched the entity draw back in fear. She knew what was happening, this power was once hers and not Jen's. Her death was eminent.

"If it was not for me, you would not have that power. It is because of my inhabiting your body. You would have never had it on your own, I added to your abilities." The entity insisted.

"That might be true. You see, I do not trust you, and I never will. You are harmful and destructive, and I feel the universe would be a much safer place if you were not in it." Jen smiled as she stared at the creature. "I guess you have worn out your welcome."

Jen pulled back her arm and took aim just as Daniel rounded the corner. "Jen, what are you doing?" Jen did not lose focus as she heard Daniel's voice, she turned loose of the energy ball and it flew forward at her intended target. With a sudden burst, the lifeforce of the entity was extinguished.

Chapter Nineteen

Life, Then Death, Then Life Again, as A Goddess

"What the hell did you do?" Daniel said as his anger grew.

"I did what I had to. I got rid of a threat that could have hurt so many innocents." Jen replied.

"Is that really the way you see it? Or were you just trying to get even with a creature that hurt you?"

"Maybe a little of both. She would have come back more powerful than before and then, who knows what she could do." Jen defended herself.

"Somewhat like yourself, I would say." Daniel was outraged.

"You may be right. I am so much more than I was before. I know that, but I am not dangerous like her. I am here for the greater good."

"The greater good does not call for unnecessary killing." Daniel said, as he began to walk away.

"Daniel please, we are together again, let's not fight. Let's agree that was an error in judgement." Jen said in a low voice, as she reached out for Daniel.

Pulling him into an embrace, Jen rested her head on Daniel's shoulder. As he pulled tight to her, Jen rotated her head. Her eyes opened wide, and the energy that filled them earlier returned. Jen smiled as she felt it race through her body. She embraced her new self.

Daniel felt unsure about the change in Jen, as they walked back to the group that awaited them. They took turns introducing themselves. Jen seemed happy to meet them all, and soon she was caught up on the situation they were all stuck in.

Amelia walked over to Daniel, who stood to the side of the group. She studied him as she got closer. Soon Zach also joined them. There was a definite feeling between them. Everyone sensed something out of place.

"OK kid, spill it. Something is wrong." Amelia blurted out.

"I feel it too. What happened?" Zach added.

"The entity is gone. Jen killed it."

"What? You mean she took its life?" Zach questioned.

"Yeah, I walked up just as she used an energy ball to wipe it out completely." Daniel felt a lump in his throat as he spoke.

"Do we have a problem here?" Amelia asked.

"I have no idea. I mean she is Jen, and I can read her just like always. Then again, she is very powerful. Not anything like before. She is like nothing I have seen before. I don't read anything from her we should be afraid of, but at the same time, she is so different." Daniel said, as he hung his head.

"Well, I guess we just have to trust her, until she gives a reason not to. Besides, if there was something wrong, you would sense it. You can still read her, can't you?" Amelia asked.

"Yeah, she still reads as the same Jen, just a little out of sorts from what happened to her."

"Then we just watch her for a while, and let her be her, until she mends a bit." Zach added.

"Yes, I am sure she will be fine." Daniel agreed.

"Who will be fine?" Jen asked as she walked up from behind.

"You will be, and if you didn't sneak up on conversations, you would not have to ask." Daniel said laughing.

"You guys do not need to worry about me. I am feeling more like myself every minute. It is just hard to shake the feeling that creature put into me."

"You have been through so much. More than one person should have to stand. So, if we are worried, it just means we love you and want you to be OK." Zach tried to smooth the situation.

"You are amazing, and I love you too. Everything will be OK. And if my power is too much for me to handle, I will come to you." Jen said confidently.

"How did you know we were worried about your powers?" Zach asked

"I sensed it in you, when we hugged. No new powers needed. That is just a leftover of my old abilities." Jen laughed at herself. "Look, I admit I was out of control, as the energy changed me and the bird appeared. But ever since, I have been calming down. I did what I had to do with the entity. She could not have been allowed to do this again, but I swear, I am OK now. No urge to kill."

Daniel stood staring at her the whole time she was talking. Secretly, he scanned every bit of her he could. Still, he sensed no danger or dishonesty. He smiled as he realized she was normal again, but deep inside he feared the energy that had been set free. If she did not stay on top of it, it could spiral out of control.

In his mind, Daniel envisioned a world being destroyed, by a goddess with no restraints. In the center of the destruction of the earth, was Jen. She never intended to attain the power that destroyed them all. In the end, Daniel would have no power to stop her. Everything and everyone they had ever known, would die at her hands. Daniel's eyes grew wide and a lump formed in his throat as he tried to shake the vision of the last days of the earth.

Chapter Twenty

The Sand Man Is Coming

Daniel tossed back and forth as the night went on. His sleep was filled with images of the end of days. He mumbled words as his head jerked back and forth. From across the room, Zach listened and pieced together what was happening. He knew what had changed Daniel's mood.

As his dream came to a climax, Daniel threw himself upwards. His bare chest was covered with sweat, as he stopped himself from screaming. His muscles flexed as he pulled himself into a tight ball. Looking around the room, he searched for Jen. She was nowhere to be seen.

Before Daniel could get up and pull on his shirt, Zach called to him. "She isn't here. She has been gone for hours. I noticed when I woke up. Mind telling me what is really going on?" Zach prodded him.

"Yeah, I would like to know that one too." Amelia called back, from her bed in the front of the plane.

"So, you both are aware?" Daniel said as he shrugged his shoulders.

"What I did not know, your dream supplied the rest." Amelia answered.

"Really, I was that loud?"

"I thought I could sleep through anything with Fred's passed out drunken snoring. Your dream was worse, and I got most of it, from you talking through it." Amelia tried to hold back her concern as she kneeled down beside Daniel.

"How bad is this?" Zach asked.

"I don't know. I just envisioned Jen destroying the world. It doesn't mean anything; I have had these visions before and they amounted to nothing."

"And you have had them before that amounted to everything, right?" Amelia added.

"Yes, you are right. I don't know what to do. And now that she has disappeared, I don't know how to take it. I mean, I scan her and she is as normal as Jen has ever been, but her power is off the charts. I don't know if she can handle that." Daniel dropped his head and sighed.

In the sky, miles away, Jen flew higher into the clouds. Her energy bird flapped its wings and she emitted a sonic scream. She enjoyed her new found power. It amazed her to feel this way, when only a couple of years ago she was a mere human and powerless. She worried about the small things like her family leaving and ending up homeless, taking refuge in a cemetery.

Her mind raced back to the moment she encountered Daniel. He became her protector. She smiled as she remembered the times they had together in the cemetery. Life was simpler then. She wondered if it was not a better place to be.

As she flew towards the sunrise, she realized she had to return to the others before they noticed she was gone. Landing just outside the door of the plane, she quietly opened it and climbed aboard, to find everyone was awake and waiting.

"Where have you been?" Daniel asked.

"I couldn't sleep and decided to go out for a while. I flew around a bit and came back. Is something wrong?" Jen asked.

"Honestly, I do not know. I read you, and it is like the same woman I fell in love with. Then you do things that make me question if you are in complete control. Then, I have visions of you destroying the earth with your new found powers. So yeah, I guess something is wrong."

"Daniel, I am totally in control. If I wasn't, I would come to you. We have been together so long; you should know I trust you with everything. If my power even started to get out of control, I would let you know. I just went out this morning for some air. It felt good to be in control again." Jen looked

Daniel straight in the eyes as she tried to comfort him.

"OK, for now. But the Jen I know and love, would have never taken the life of the entity." Daniel spoke before he thought of what he was saying.

"She, …I would have, if it meant doing so would protect my friends. I would never want to know, that letting that creature live, meant allowing one of you to come to harm. I had simply had enough, and the violation of my body and the fear of what it could do next. I did not buy the innocent routine she was selling. What she did to me inside and out, was in no way innocent." Jen fumed.

Jen turned her head away as she tried to hold back her tears. Daniel felt her pain through their rapport. She was telling the truth. He breathed deeply knowing she was not holding anything back.

As Jen calmed down, she turned back to them in a frantic state. Her senses were screaming in her head. Something was wrong. She could feel the impending danger. Turning to Daniel, she grabbed tight to his hand, and spoke. "They're here."

"Who is here? What do you mean?" He asked.

"I can sense things now. I know things that are happening around me. I can sense a sandman. He is here in this area, searching for us."

"Do you know exactly where?" Zach asked.

"He is coming this way, towards the plane. He can't find us here." Jen said beginning to panic.

"Calm down, I will go outside and take care of him. If he doesn't see you, he will not know you are here." Amelia said as she walked to the door of the plane.

Down on the ground the sandman approached. He was in full gear including the computerized goggles, sand bag and jumpsuit. Amelia studied him as she closed the door to the plane. He reminded her of an aviator from days past. She smiled as she tried to envision him as a threat.

'Can I help you with something?" She called out.

"I am looking for three people who might have travelled here. Two boys and a girl, all around twenty years old." The sandman studied Amelia as he spoke.

"Can't say I have seen anyone new here in a while." She responded.

The sandman looked at her hard, trying to decide if he believed her. Amelia had a good poker face, and he knew only one way to be sure. Reaching to his side pouch, he drew out a handful of the sand he carried. Before Amelia could duck and run, he threw the dust over her.

Amelia's eyes glazed over as the sand entered her skin and began to take control. She could not struggle, it would do no good, the sand was all powerful, and she was a mere human. She just stood there like a dime store mannequin.

"Now let's try this again." The sandman said feeling sure of himself.

"Who is on the plane?"

"My co-pilot Fred Nunan. He is sleeping off a night of being drunk." Amelia answered.

"Have you seen the ones I asked about." He demanded.

"I might have, but there are so many people coming in around here. It is hard to say." Amelia answered him with a frozen gaze upon her face.

"Fine, I am done with you now." He said as he began to walk away.

Inside the plane the others watched until he was out of sight. Jen held tight to Daniel as she stared into the distance. Daniel slowly opened the door and looked around to make sure it was safe. Then they joined Amelia on the ground.

"How did she defy the sandman like that." Zach asked.

"It should not have been possible for her to lie to him." Daniel said as he stared into Amelia's eyes.

"Who said I lied?" Amelia said laughing.

"But you told him we were not here." Jen responded to her.

"No, I said Fred was onboard drunk. Which he is, and I said a lot of people come here. I never lied; I just chose what truth I told him." Amelia smiled as she put an arm around Jen.

"We have to get out of here and see what is happening with the invasion." Daniel spoke up.

"Yes, they obviously know you are here. More will come."

"Well, we know where there is a portal, and I have these nifty new powers. I bet I could rip the doorway open enough for us to get out." Jen said feeling proud of herself."

"Yeah, but not all of us can go." Amelia added.

"Then, we go first, and prepare to come back for you all. We will find a way to take you back to earth, I promise." Daniel felt sure he would find a way.

Afterwards

Jen looked around them and searched for a way to support the boys in their journey out. Near them, stretched out on the ground was a metal platform that was thick enough to support two men's weight.

As she walked towards it, the piece of metal rose from the ground. As it climbed upwards, shiny streams of sand fell to the ground, all around where it had been.   Jen walked over and observed her choice. She was pleased.

Allowing the metal to float just a couple of feet above the ground, she motioned for the boys to climb on top. It held them quite well. Daniel turned to look back at Amelia. He felt guilty for leaving her there.

"I will be back for you soon. I promise you." He said sincerely.

"I know you will. I trust you. Always will." She said back to him, as she waved goodbye, and blew a kiss.

"Hang on guys. It's time to go." Jen said, as she erected a shield around them, and she pulled the metal platform. She took them upwards, with her bright golden energy bird, headed towards the portal opening.

As they arrived, Jen forced the door to open, and they ascended into the attached wormhole. Jen remembered how they ended up there, and this time, she felt certain she could guide them to safety.

They slid through the gateway back towards the sandman universe. As they landed on the ground near the sand factory, Jen lowered her shield, and they ran for the building to see if the invasion had begun.

Daniel orbed just inside the doorway, and unlocked it for Jen and Zach to follow. Inside they found the place very much as they had left it before. The invasion had not begun, but by the looks of everything, they were ready.

"Notify the Queen, the scouts have been sent. When they send word back, we will be ready to begin to spread the red sand." A worker called out over a distant radio.

Daniel looked at Jen. "We are too late. As soon as they spread the sand over the earth, every living thing will be dead."

<u>Continued in</u>

Dream Walker Book Three:

Conquest of the Sandman

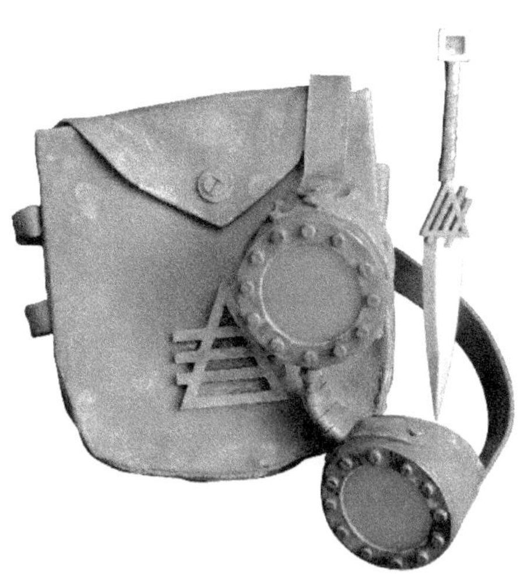

Thanks for choosing this book, if you enjoyed it,
please leave positive feedback.

**Included at the end of this book, are the first two
chapters of G.W. Mullins' Best-Selling title
Nick Grainger Book One The Curse Of Cleopatra**

Daniel walked
in the land of
the dead.
Now the dead
want him
back!

For Information About

From The Dead
Of Night

The Book Series Visit
gwmullins.wixsite.com/books

About the Author

G.W. Mullins is an Author, Photographer, and Entrepreneur of Native American / Cherokee descent. He has been a published author for over 10 years. His writing has focused on the paranormal and Native American studies. Mullins has released several books on the history/stories/fables of the Native American Indians.

Among his books are the extremely successful ***Star People, Sky Gods, And Other Tales Of The Native American Indians***, ***The Native American Story Book - Stories Of The American Indians For Children Volumes 1-5***, ***The Native American Cookbook***, and ***Walking With Spirits Native American Myths, Legends, And Folklore Volumes 1 Thru 6***.

He has released the complete series from his Sci/fi Fantasy Series ***From The Dead Of Night***, including the Best-Selling titles - ***Daniel Is Waiting***, and ***Daniel Returns***.

His most recent work includes the new series ***Rise Of The Snow Queen*** featuring ***Book One The Polar Bear King***, and ***Book Two The War Of The Witches***. He has also released ***Messages from The Other Side*** a nonfiction book about communication with the dead.

For further information, on his writing, visit G.W. Mullins' web site at ***http://gwmullins.wix.com/books***.

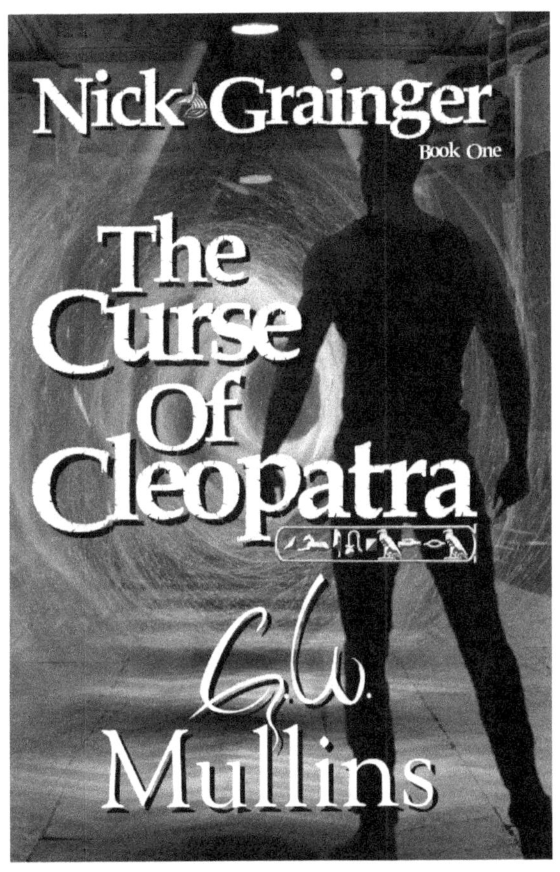

Nick Grainger Book One The Curse Of Cleaoptra Is Available in Hardback (978-1-7377100-8-0), Paperback (978-1-7377100-9-7) and various eBook formats worldwide.

NICK GRAINGER
BOOK ONE
THE CURSE OF CLEOPATRA

"everything has its balance—in madness is much wisdom, and in wisdom much madness."
— **H. Rider Haggard, Cleopatra**

Before

The sounds of fighting filled the area all about her, as Cleopatra lifted herself from her golden throne. As she paced, her mind raced, as she feverishly sought a way out of her impending doom.

As she turned on her heels, she spoke aloud. "I will not give in to the Romans. I will not be a prisoner to be paraded around by Octavian as a trophy of his conquest. I would rather die before this dishonor."

She threw her head back as she studied the walls of her chamber. There was no escape for her this time. As she contemplated her final moves, she thought back on her life. Cleopatra had been blood-thirsty in her acquisition of royalty. Not much more than a murderer, she had been prepared to remove anyone who stood in her way.

Moving back to her throne, she slid comfortably to her seat and called for her servants. Two women entered the chamber, they knew why they were there, and what Cleopatra had asked for. As they approached, the older of the two kneeled at her feet, and held out the woven basket to her.

"Is it what I asked for?" Cleopatra asked.

"Yes, my queen. An asp, as poisonous as any that could be found." The older woman replied.

"Yes, but how do I know this is true. I would not dare allow this creature to bite me and its promise not be fulfilled." Cleopatra looked down at the kneeling woman, with a crazed look on her face. "You will show me of its power, put your hand in the basket."

"No, my queen, I beg of you!" The woman cried out.

"How dare you tell me no. I am the Queen of Egypt and until I depart this world, you will obey me."

Cleopatra rose to her feet and pulled out a knife from her breastplate. As she lunged forward, she found her mark in the woman's neck, slicing her carotid artery. Blood flew forth in waves as it coated the steps leading from the throne. As the basket fell in front of the woman, Cleopatra grasped it in her hands.

As she turned around, she looked at the young girl servant. "So, my pretty one, it seems you have two options, die at my hands, or gently fade away from the poison of the asp. You decide."

The girl shook in fear as she studied the room. She had no way out. As she looked into the desperate eyes of her Queen, she decided her fate. She reached out her arm as she drew closer to Cleopatra. Without saying a word, she offered her life in the test if the creatures poison.

"I do this because I have no other choice. It is not because I am loyal to you." The girl's voice echoed her disgust.

"Save your breath, I do not care what you think. In the end, you will serve your queen whether you like it or not."

As the girl's arm reached the basket, Cleopatra released the rope that kept it closed. Then taking hold of the girl, she forced her hand inside. The creature, already enraged buy the constant movement of the basket, struck hard driving its venom deep into her skin.

As the girl fell to the floor she stared in the eyes of her murderer. "You may not pay in this life. But in the next, I wish you nothing but pain and torment." As the girl's voice trailed off, she slowly fell to her side. The poison had worked, she was dead.

Cleopatra walked over and looked at the girl as her lifeless body lay on the floor. As she kneeled beside her, Cleopatra took a deep breath. A tear ran from her eye as she stroked the girl's hair. "You were such a beautiful young thing. I was as beautiful as you once."

As cleopatra pulled the girl into her lap, her demeanor changed. She seemed motherly and caring. Her mind raced from state to state. She was unstable, perhaps bordering on psychotic. She cried as she held the girl. Fear gripped her as she realized there was little time left.

Turning to the older woman, she studied her. "If I changed your clothing, and applied makeup to your face, you could be made to look as I do." She talked to herself as she prepared the body of the older woman. Dressing her in fine clothing and changing her hair, she created a very good likeness of herself.

Grabbing ahold of the woman, she dragged her lifeless body to a bench a few feet from her. "I may have to allow you to impersonate me, but I will be damned if you do it on my throne." Then she pulled the younger girl to the side of the seat and positioned her alongside. She laughed out loud as she studied the scene she had set. "A murder suicide if I have ever seen one." She said as she placed the knife she had used earlier beside the girl.

As she turned to leave the chamber, she moved behind her throne, and reached to the back where a hidden compartment was. Inside she pulled out a set of colored crystals. Each different in color and size, they all had a particular purpose.

Cleopatra moved quickly through the complex, avoiding all that might see her. As she entered the final chamber, in a darkened corner was a table in front of a large obelisk. She moved quickly, as she laid the crystals out on the table and began to arrange them in a particular order.

As she placed the last red colored crystal in position, a light began to emit from inside the pyramid shaped opening. A gateway of light formed in the front of the structure. Then a light blasted forward in a blinding beam, as it quieted and Cleopatra moved forward. She turned to look around her as she prepared to enter. "Until I return." She said laughing as she climbed through the opening and was gone as the light disappeared.

Chapter One: Egypt Present Day

Nick couldn't help the smile on his face as he approached the great pyramid. He had dreamed of this his whole life. He had never believed he would be able to explore this, or any other ancient ruin, but when his professor offered the opportunity to go to Egypt, he knew he could not refuse.

Professor Newton was a well-known archeologist, and very respected in his field. He had been trying for years to arrange an expedition of ruins in Egypt, but with all the unrest in the area, his university refused to allow the trip. When the climate had settled and seemed to be safer, he pitched his idea again. This time, the committee who had rejected him so many times, had no choice to approve his request and allow for two of his top students to travel with him as well.

The professor chose Nick Grainger, his top student as his first choice. Nick had excelled at everything since he entered the university at the age of 16. He had already completed a degree in science when he chose to continue in the field of Archeology on his 20th birthday. Nick was probably one of the brightest students in the whole school, but lacked direction.

The second student the professor chose was Emma Blunt. Emma was 19, and a very pretty girl and a brilliant student. She was enthusiastic in her studies, and the runner up student in the department. She always seemed to come in second to Nick, and everyone was beginning to notice her resentment to him. The professor was hoping the expedition would somehow bring a little peace between them.

As Nick studied the stones that made up the giant pyramid, he did not notice that the professor and Emma had come up behind him. "Impressive, isn't it?" The professor asked.

"Amazing!" Nick replied. "I am overwhelmed. I never thought it would be so close I could touch it."

The professor laughed, "Then touch it and get a feel of the last ancient wonder of the world, the Great Pyramid of Giza." They all stepped back as they looked to the top of the pyramid in amazement of its size.

"What's on the agenda for the day professor?" Emma said catching her breath.

"I thought today we would tour a few places and get a feel for the Ancients. Then tomorrow we begin exploring a new hidden chamber that was discovered just before we came here."

As they moved inside the pyramid, the professor led them on a guided tour. Nick was in awe of the sites and the antiquity of everything he saw. His mind raced to try to understand why the place was built and how someone in ancient Egypt designed it. In his mind, he was sure there was some alien history behind everything. He had seen a television show that said the pyramid was a part of a network of power stations. He liked this idea.

The group moved on from location to location, seeing the tombs that had been opened to the public as well as some areas that were not. The whole experience was so much to take in, that when they arrived back at their hotel, everyone was exhausted. Going their separate ways, they all settled in for the night.

As the night grew later, Nick ventured out to the vending area and ice machine, trying to get something cold to drink. As he rounded the corner, he saw her standing there. He studied Emma, she was beautiful, but so out of his league. He thought about it, but knew they had been at each other's throats since they met.

Emma studied the options in the machine. She wanted chocolate, but the machine was loaded with things she did not know or want to know of. She turned to the side and looked at the next machine, she caught a glimpse of Nick. She had always had a weird attraction to him, even though on most days she could not stand him. She didn't know how to explained it, but he was cute in his own nerdy way. And for her that worked.

Nick cleared his throat, as he prepared to approach her. "Anything good in there?" He asked as he stared over her shoulder.

"I have no idea; I don't recognize any of this." Emma replied. "I guess I am out of luck, because there is no way I am venturing out into the streets at night around here."

"I'll go for you. What do you want?" He asked.

"I just wanted chocolate, but it's no big deal."

"I'll get it for you." Nick said as he turned to walk away.

"Why would you do anything for me? I thought you hated me." She questioned him.

"Well, maybe because, we are here for the next few weeks and we need to find a way to get along. Also, I agree, you should not be out on those streets at night. So, I will go for you."

"Thanks Nick." She said as he walked away.

Later that night, Emma sat in her room trying to get the internet to work with the poor reception of the hotel. As she was about to give up and put it aside, she heard a knock at her door.

Opening it, she saw a bag on the floor, as she looked in, there were several candy bars, of all different types inside. Nick had fulfilled his promise. She saw the figure of a boy rounding the corner as she looked for him. If he had stayed, he would have seen the huge smile on her face. Peace had been found.

As Emma sat upon her bed, she pulled out her cell phone and looked for Nick's number. She was sure she had it, since all the classmates had shared numbers earlier that year. Then she found it on the list. She pulled up the text screen and started to type. Mid-sentence she stopped. No, she thought, there was a better way. She searched through until she found an emoji with a huge smiling face. She decided it was perfect, and it was sent. She sat back against a pillow on her bed and unwrapped some of her chocolate and smiled.

Mullins

Dream Walker Book Two

<u>Also Available From G.W. Mullins</u>

Rise Of The Snow Queen Book Two The War Of The Witches

Daniel Awakens A Ghost Story Begins– From The Dead Of Night Prequel

Daniel Is Waiting A Ghost Story – From The Dead Of Night Book One

Daniel Returns A Ghost Story - From The Dead Of Night Book Two

Daniel's Fate A Ghost Story Ends - From The Dead Of Night Book Four

Rise Of The Snow Queen Book One The Polar Bear King

Messages From The Other Side Stories of the Dead, Their Communication, and Unfinished Business

Vengeance

Mysteries Of The Unseen World – Ghost, Hauntings and The Unexplained

Haunted America Stories Of Ghost, Hauntings And
The Unexplained

Timeless – A Paranormal Romance Murder Mystery

Star People, Sky Gods, And Other Tales Of The
Native American Indians

More Star People, Sky Gods, And Other Paranormal
Tales Of The Native American Indians

Lost Tales Of The Native American Indians Vol 1

Walking With Spirits Native American Myths,
Legends, And Folklore Volumes One Thru Six

The Native American Cookbook

Native American Cooking - An Indian Cookbook
With Legends And Folklore

The Native American Story Book - Stories Of The
American Indians For Children
Volumes One Thru Five

The Best Native American Stories For Children

Dream Walker Book Two

Cherokee A Collection of American Indian Legends, Stories And Fables

Creation Myths - Tales Of The Native American Indians

Strange Tales Of The Native American Indians

Spirit Quest - Stories Of The Native American Indians

Animal Tales Of The Native American Indians

Medicine Man - Shamanism, Natural Healing, Remedies And Stories Of The Native American Indians
Native American Legends: Stories Of The Hopi Indians Volumes One and Two

Totem Animals Of The Native Americans

The Best Native American Myths, Legends And Folklore Volumes One Thru Three

Ghosts, Spirits And The Afterlife In Native American Indian Mythology And Folklore

War Song: Tales Of The Native American Indians

Origin Tales Of The Native American